H. m.

I've travelled the world twice over,
Met the famous: saints and sinners,
Poets and artists, kings and queens,
Old stars and hopeful beginners,
I've been where no-one's been before,
Learned secrets from writers and cooks
All with one library ticket
To the wonderful world of books.

AFTER MIDNIGHT

Sharon Denholm went to Warden's Cove in search of Brent Warden and found that Brent was a widower whose wife had died in suspicious circumstances a year before. There she met his beautiful sister-in-law who had been crippled in the accident, his strange, devoted Aunt, his wild brother and his son. Also on the property is station hand, Hank, who has not long been out of prison. Did Brent kill his wife? Sharon is determined to find out but she realises that she is putting herself in the dead woman's shoes and she has become the potential victim of a murderer.

EVA BURFIELD

AFTER MIDNIGHT

Complete and Unabridged

ULVERSCROFT
Leicester

First published in Great Britain in 1965 by
Wright & Brown Ltd.,
London

First Large Print Edition
published July 1987

British Library CIP Data

Burfield, Eva
    After midnight.—Large print ed.—
Ulverscroft large print series: romance
I. Title
823'.914[F]   PR6052.U62/

ISBN 0-7089-1651-1

Published by
F. A. Thorpe (Publishing) Ltd.
Anstey, Leicestershire
Set by Rowland Phototypesetting Ltd.
Bury St. Edmunds, Suffolk
Printed and bound in Great Britain by
T. J. Press (Padstow) Ltd., Padstow, Cornwall

To
Nola and Roy and their children
Derek, Gary, Pam and Yvonne

1

ALL her life Sharon would remember that night.

It was a lovely mellow summer evening, quite in keeping with her mood, but it was almost too warm and she was quite unaware of the thunder clouds gathering over the hills towards the coast. After dinner the family were driven outside by the heat inside which would not be dispelled by the wide open doors and windows. They gathered on the veranda at the front of the house; her mother and father sharing the colonial couch under the bedroom window and her twenty-year-old sister sitting on the step. Immediately below the step, the path and the lawn dropped away to the street; a quiet, twisting, hilly street, with few houses and heavily lined with foliage.

Sharon, too, wandered out to join them; expectant, a little nervous. She stood in the doorway and looked at the asphalt strip of road, curving away out of sight. In a short time Brent would appear; driving his long, cream station wagon, or striding along the narrow strip of footpath. He will be wearing his dark green suit, she told herself, with a white shirt and a narrow tie. Though she was rather disinterested in clothes for herself and inclined not to worry about appearances, it pleased her that he dressed well and correctly. He always knew the right thing to say, the right thing to do, the right thing to wear, and this made it even more flattering that he should be attracted to her. His brown hair will be smooth and in place, she thought on, dreamily. It almost exactly matches the colour of his skin. Sometimes his green-brown eyes will smile and sometimes they will be serious. He will tower over Dad when he shakes hands with him and Mother will look like a midget beside him. Perhaps he will push back one side of his jacket and put one hand, only one, never two, in his pocket, the way he does. It makes him look so relaxed. He will be much more relaxed than any of us.

Bob Denholm sat forward on the colonial couch and peered down the road. "And where is this boy-friend of yours?"

he asked, with just a hint of amusement in his voice.

Sharon looked at her waatch. "It's a bit early yet. We agreed he should come at half past seven."

"If he comes at all."

Sharon turned round to look at her sister. Kerry stared back. There was the faintest, spiteful light in her beautiful, wide blue eyes. She was leaning back against the veranda post, her ash-blonde hair piled upon her head in an elaborate bee-hive. Sharon could see that she had been to the hairdresser only that day for there was a brightness, a shine, a smoothness about her hair at that moment that seldom lasted more than a few hours after a trip to the salon. But it was more than just her hair. Kerry was dressed up. She was wearing an eye-catching green sheath frock, sheerest nylons and coffee-coloured court shoes. At this time of the day she generally lounged around the house in matador trousers, and Sharon was suspicious. Does she think she can take him off me like all the others? she wondered, and felt a little tingle of alarm in the pit of her stomach.

3

Somehow she had thought Brent would be too old to interest the twenty-year-old Kerry. He was thirty-six. But I'm only two years older than Kerry, she reminded herself, and he is attractive to me.

She had been attracted to him the very first time she had seen him. He had come into the bank where she worked to cash some travellers' cheques. She had been working in the Bills Department and it fell to her to serve him. He was not in any hurry and they talked lightly about the weather. Somewhere in the conversation he had told her he wanted to do some fishing while he spent a few days in the town. Though fishing was beyond her personal experience she loved the outdoors and could tell him about all the beaches, the river, and the most likely places to make a catch.

The next afternoon he came back to tell her that he had caught "a tremendous trout" that morning and that the hotel cook was cooking it for dinner that night. He insisted that she dine with him and share his triumph and they had dined together in the town's one hotel. From this gay beginning their relationship had developed over the last few weeks. Tonight was a climax; the first time he would meet her family.

If he comes at all, Kerry had said.

"Of course he'll come," Hilda Denholm, her mother, answered. "Why shouldn't he come?"

"Sometimes I think he doesn't exist at all," Kerry murmured. "The way Sharon keeps him hidden."

"I have not kept him hidden." Sharon was quick to defend herself but she was not entirely happy. Had she really kept him hidden almost without knowing it herself? Was she, even after these last weeks, unsure of him, afraid that Kerry might once again work the magic and entice him away, that her overwhelming sex appeal might attract Brent even though he had shown such interest in Sharon who considered herself plain?

She stared down at the shabby blue jeans she was wearing with a faded shirt-blouse, and her mother seemed to sense what she was thinking. "Sharon, dear, why don't you go in and change? Your young man will be here any time and you're not ready."

Sharon had not intended to change. She wanted Brent to see her with her family as she really was. She had not consciously dressed up for him once in the last few weeks and he had liked her as she was; in a plain linen suit at work, these same jeans and brief top at the beach at the week-end, and a straight, unadorned frock in the evenings.

"Put a frock on, dear, and some stockings," Hilda went on.

She had not worn stockings once this summer.

"And do something with your hair."

She was about to retort that her hair was how she liked it, but, at that moment, she looked down into her mother's concerned eyes and realized that Hilda was afraid for her. In her mother's eyes Sharon was just as precious as her prettier, younger daughter and she was afraid she would get hurt.

She ran her hand through her hair in a boyish gesture. Her hair was always just a bit too long because she hated the fuss of getting it cut, she went to the salon only when it was absolutely necessary and the family could no longer stand seeing it all over her face, being brushed awkwardly out of her eyes or caught casually at the back with a round clip to keep it out of the way. Without a word she went back into the house and into her bedroom.

The bedroom was like Sharon herself, clean, practical, without any decoration at all, and rather untidy. No matter how hard she tried there always seemed to be something lying around waiting to be put away. The frock she had worn all day at the bank lay over the bed. She wished vaguely that she had hung it up because it looked rather crumpled and screwed up and would probably need ironing before it could be worn again. But she had been in such a hurry after dinner to get out into the garden and finish weeding the strawberry bed. She looked ruefully at her fingernails and wished she had thought of wearing her mother's gardening gloves. There was a fine half-moon of dirt under each nail. She crossed the hall into the bathroom and ran some water into the basin. But Kerry had been an hour in the bath that evening and there was no hot water. She scrubbed at her nails in the cold water. She hated dirt but the way of life she preferred made it hard to keep clean.

Back in the bedroom she rummaged in the wardrobe for another dress, pulled it over her slim, five-foot-six figure and belted it round her narrow waist. She stared at herself in the mirror over the dressing-table. What to do with her hair? She could think of nothing other than to clip it off her face with two tortoiseshell combs. She studied her brown face with the dark-wing eyebrows and chocolate-coloured eyes. She was not at all like Kerry, who had fine, patrician features and very fair colouring. Sharon's face was fuller, her features not so finely drawn. It was an attractive face, quiet and honest in expression, a face quick to smile, but, because she had always compared herself to her sister, she really believed it was plain. And it was devoid of make-up, she had no tricks to conceal any small defects. A little lipstick was all she could ever be bothered with. There was nothing on the top of the dressing-table other than a brush and comb and a book on gardening. For a moment she sighed for the equipment in Kerry's room, but the mood passed. She could never for long concentrate on herself.

She hastened back to the veranda, afraid that he may have arrived while she was not there to greet him, but only her family was there making desultory conversation and relaxing in the heat.

"Ah, that's better, dear," her mother greeted her.

Sharon wandered down the steps of the veranda to the garden, glancing along the street to see if he was coming. Absent-mindedly, to keep herself occupied and her emotions under control, she stooped to pull an odd weed or two from the soil.

"Oh, don't do that, dear," Hilda exclaimed. "You'll get your clothes dirty."

She dropped the weeds as if they were hot and put both her hands behind her like a naughty child, remembering the dirty finger-nails.

Kerry stood up and stretched her hands over her head. She was beautifully proportioned and even Sharon could not help looking at her with admiration.

"Well, when is this boy-friend of yours going to show up?"

Sharon controlled her temper with

difficulty. She had taught herself years before not to answer Kerry back. It only developed into a violent quarrel and upset Hilda.

"He'll be here in a minute."

The three pairs of eyes looked at her and she was disconcerted. She went back up the veranda steps and faced them.

"Look, please . . ." She shrugged helplessly. "Be nice to him . . . I mean . . . don't take him too much for granted. We're not serious . . ."

That was a lie. She was serious. But was Brent? She had a thousand sudden pictures of him in the last few weeks. Laughing at the beach with a backdrop of sea and sky; brown and hard and muscular in the sun. And in the picture theatre, the homely, pleasant profile against the faintly lit far wall; the time he caught her watching him and grinned quietly, enclosing them in their own secret little circle. The day he came into the bank to see her, formal and correct, while the other girls discussed him as they talked.

"And what does this young man do for a living?" Bob Denholm asked, suddenly becoming the conscientious father.

10

"Oh, Dad, I don't know. I haven't asked him."

"Well, where does he live?"

"At the hotel."

"That's not an address. Where's his home?"

"I don't know. He's just passing through. He's on holiday."

"It's a very long holiday. He's been here for weeks, hasn't he?"

"Well, he didn't intend staying so long, but after we met and . . . well, he keeps putting it off . . . going away I mean . . ."

"And hasn't the fellow told you where he lives?"

"No."

"That seems odd," her father persisted.

"He . . . he *did* say once that he lived somewhere up North . . ."

How could she explain to them that these things had been unimportant, they could wait. They had both been living for the moment ever since they met. But she was perturbed. She wanted to know everything about him, everything. Had he avoided discussing these things with her?

"I think he's a myth," Kerry murmured.

"Don't be silly," Sharon answered, sharply.

"Well, where is he?" Kerry looked at her watch. "It's nearly eight o'clock."

"Now, Kerry," Bob Denholm interrupted. "You know what men are, specially when they get stuck in a pub. He's probably in the bar and can't get away."

Sharon looked down the road again, wishing he would appear at that very moment.

At nine o'clock he still had not come, and they all moved indoors again.

2

THEY were all very silent at breakfast the next morning. Hilda Denholm ached with sympathy for her daughter. If it had been Kerry she would not have worried. Kerry was always involved with one man or another and would take this situation lightly, but Sharon was different. Sharon had not shown an interest in a man for a long time. Hilda did not realize that Sharon had become just a little bitter about men and avoided becoming emotionally involved because each time she had introduced a man to her family he had somehow become just another boy-friend of Kerry's. Bob Denholm, who had overnight developed into an old-fashioned father, was vocal.

"I'd like to teach that blighter a thing or two."

His wife frowned at him. "It might have been unavoidable. He'll probably phone this morning and apologize."

Even Kerry was moved to sympathy for Sharon. After her half-serious, half-in-fun teasing of the night before, she had the grace to feel a little bit ashamed.

"Why don't you ring the hotel and ask him what happened?" she suggested.

But Sharon, who was not used to Kerry showing her any understanding misunderstood, thought Kerry was sneering at her, and ignored her.

She was utterly bewildered. Could he have mistaken the night? But she had seen him in the afternoon and he had said, "See you about seven-thirty." There was only the faint hope that he would telephone today and apologize and explain.

Each time the telephone rang at work that morning her heart thumped uncomfortably. But she was not called to the telephone. As twelve o'clock drew near she knew she would have to go home and face the family and admit that he had not rung. In desperation she slipped into the telephone booth in the office and dialled the hotel.

"Is Mr. Warden there?" she asked the proprietor when he answered her ring.

"Warden? Nope. He checked out."

"Oh."

"Yes. Early yesterday evening. Sorry."

"Thank you."

She hung up slowly and it took all her courage to go back into the banking chamber and control her expression. So he had gone without a word rather than meet her family. Why? Because meeting the family was a final step? An admission? But I'm sure he loves me, she told herself. Was he, perhaps, already married? I must think, I must think this out, she insisted to herself.

She went back to her desk and sat down, staring at the ledger in front of her without seeing it. The bank was sombre and silent except for the click of a book-keeping machine. She began to go over the last few weeks in her mind trying to remember everything, all the little things that he had said and done, looking for a clue that would explain his sudden departure. But there was nothing. He had acted like any ordinary young man meeting a girl on a holiday and gradually growing more and more interested in her.

The thought of her family's sympathy was almost too much to bear. She had a

15

deep inner pride and it hurt. And she was convinced that Brent had been sincere. I won't just sit around and lose him like that, she thought desperately. She was fiercely independent, not given to self-pity, never expecting the gods to be kind. Subconsciously, she believed that heaven helps those who help themselves.

After a while the despair began to give way to anger. How dare he do this to her? Embarrass her in front of her friends and family. But when she thought clearly about him, the anger softened. Why did you do it, Brent? she asked the ledger page. Where are you?

This thought gave her an idea and she went into the strong-room and leafed through a file. Which day had he come into the bank to cash his cheques? She felt a little breathless when she found the entry. The travellers' cheques had been issued in a place called Te Kiri. But where on earth was Te Kiri? There was a large map of New Zealand on one wall of the banking chamber and she went and stood in front of it and studied it quietly. It took a long time to find Te Kiri. It was a very small, black speck somewhere on the East Coast of the North Island.

She studied the map carefully. One would have to take a train up the main trunk to start on a journey to Te Kiri. That would mean catching the evening rail car. But I'm not going to Te Kiri, she argued. That may not be his home at all. Just because he bought travellers' cheques in Te Kiri did not mean he lived there. But it was a clue, a starting-off place.

Her mind was crystal clear suddenly. It would not be lady-like to seek Brent in Te Kiri or anywhere when he had so abruptly deserted her, but this did not disconcert her. I'm never very lady-like anyway, she told herself. There was a question here to which she must find an answer or it would haunt her all her life. But she would not tell anyone where she was going in case they tried to stop her. Fortunately, she was to start her annual leave at the beginning of the following week and she would ask the manager if it could be put forward a day or two. She would tell her family that she was going away for her holidays just as she usually did. They would be sympathetic. They would understand and

17

think she just wanted to get away quickly after her disappointment. If it could be arranged, she would be on the rail car the next night.

3

THE ungainly bus came to a stop in the main street of Te Kiri. It was early evening and the hot white summer sun was still high in the heavens. Sharon was the only passenger in the bus other than the schoolchildren returning home from school in the larger town ten miles back along the dusty road.

As soon as the driver pushed open the door the children spilled out into the roadway. There were about fifteen of them and Sharon waited for them to pass before she, too, went down the bus steps and into the street. The driver lifted her one, small suitcase out for her.

"There you are. That's as far as I go. Te Kiri."

"Oh . . ."

Sharon stood on the hard-baked, dusty road and surveyed the township. There were no footpaths. The two shops, a general store and a small drapery, two high wooden buildings with corrugated-iron veranda roofs to shelter the window-shopper, were built on the edge of the road itself. A little further along another high wooden building leaned on tip-toe at the street's edge. Sharon could see the words "Te Kiri Hotel" painted underneath the upstairs' windows.

The bus driver was unloading parcels and bundles of newspapers.

"That's the pub along there," he told her. "They'll be able to put you up if you want a room."

"Oh, yes. Thanks . . ."

She moved a little way down the street and again stood still and studied the town. The few shops and commercial buildings lined the road which, only a short distance away, swept down to the sea. From where Sharon stood she could see a triangle of deep, green-blue sea and milky-blue sky. The town sat in a valley, unplanned, its buildings sprinkled without thought among the trees and bushes. There were not many. Opposite the hotel was a sprawling garage with a car and a truck outside, next door a small, more-modern building proclaimed itself to be the Bank of New Zealand Agency. At the foot of the nearest hills Sharon could see a homely church spire. There were one or two houses with neat gardens close to the main street and several could be seen scattered about the first range of hills.

She moved on to the hotel. Beneath the veranda that fronted the street two or three men, Maoris and pakehas, sat on wooden forms, drinking. An open window gave a view of the bar where a man in his shirt sleeves was methodically wiping glasses between serving the customers. The front door was wide open and somewhere inside a radio was playing loudly.

Carrying her small suitcase (she was a person given to travelling lightly and boasted she could go away for a week with less luggage than Kerry used overnight) Sharon moved past the men and into the lobby of the hotel. Except for the men she could glimpse in the bar, there was no sign of life. The hall was all match-lining with one cubicle partitioned off and the word "Office" painted on the door. On one side there was a push-bell with "Please ring" printed underneath. After a moment she pushed the bell experimentally.

She waited and soon a woman appeared

21

from the deep bowels of the building. She was a big woman with a head of wiry red hair, and she wore a floral apron over a cotton frock, and shabby slippers.

Sharon smiled pleasantly; her infectious smile.

"Hello."

The woman ran a hand through her thick hair. "Hello. Now where have I seen you before . . . ?"

A little taken aback, Sharon replied, "I . . . I don't think you've ever seen me . . ."

"No. Well, maybe not. You don't live around here, that's for sure."

"No. I've just come up for a few days and I'd like a room please."

"Well, we got plenty of those. You should see the proprietor, but he's in the bar at the moment. I only work here. However, I guess I can take you up. Can you manage that bag?"

"Oh, yes. Yes, thank you."

"I'd help you with it, but I get arthritis in my shoulders something awful. Got to be careful . . ."

"That's all right. It isn't heavy at all."

The woman moved off to the foot of a

flight of stairs and began an awkward ascent talking loudly all the time. Sharon followed.

"Don't know why anyone would want to come here for a few days. Not unless you're plumb crazy about the sea. It's the only thing around here. Nothing to do. No shops to speak of, no pictures, television hasn't hit us yet. There's only the beach and fishing, and you can only do that when the tide's right. I like my beaches civilized, a stone's throw from a good town, shops right on the sand as you might say, lawns and gardens and a sound-shell with concerts. What do you say?"

"I don't know. I haven't thought about it," Sharon answered, wryly, wondering why the woman bothered to live in such an out-of-the-way spot if she disliked it so.

At the top of the stairs they came out into a long corridor with rooms opening off both sides.

"The bedrooms are all on this floor," the woman went on. "Don't suppose it matters much which one you have. No one here but the permanents, hardly ever is. And the staff of course."

She pushed open the first door and

exposed a clean enough room, plainly furnished. "How about this one?"

"That'll do, thanks."

"You'll have to sign on when the boss is in the office." She shrugged. "Well, have fun. There's nothing to do around here . . ."

"I've . . . I've come to see some . . . friends. I wonder if you can tell me where they live." Sharon hesitated. "Warden is their name."

"Warden? Huh. I know that bunch all right, all right. They're an odd lot and that's for sure. You don't want to get too mixed up with them."

Sharon was immediately on the defensive for Brent. Apparently Warden was his real name and this made her fiercely partisan. Somehow she had expected it to be an alias. But he had not lied and this added to his sincerity and made her feel that her errand was justified.

"I don't know what you mean," she answered, coldly.

"Then you can't know them very well. You think that silly old Dorothy Warden isn't a queer 'un? And that Brent's been acting very odd since his wife died . . ."

"Oh . . ." Sharon went cold with the sudden shock. Since his wife died. That he might be married had already occurred to her; it would have explained his sudden departure. But this was something different.

"Mind you he never was that sociable. Living way out there the way they do, I suppose. Used to come into town, but never into the bar for a drink. Everybody else does, even Doctor Matthews stops off for a spot now and again, but Brent Warden, no. Thinks he's too good for the rest of us, I guess. Aloof, that's what he is. Just does his business and off again."

"Would you mind telling me where they live? How I can get there?"

"You won't be able to get there till tomorrow now. The boat only makes one trip a day four times a week. Unless there's someone in town from one of the other bays with their own boat . . ."

"Boat? Where do they live?"

"Place called Warden's Cove. 'Bout ten miles along the coast!"

"Perhaps I could get a car . . . ?"

"Can't get there by car. There's no road. Can't get there anyway 'cept by boat.

If the tide's out you can walk along the beach and just make it round the cliffs, but that's a pretty long walk."

"But surely there's some way . . ."

"Look out of the window if you don't believe me. There's the ranges in the way. Mind you there's some good farm land on the other side but it backs up against those hills and nobody's put a road through yet. There's all sorts of arguments going on with the Ministry of Works to get one, so that them that live on the other side can get in and out by road, but it could go on for years."

Sharon moved across to a window which overlooked the main street and she could see that the foothills did indeed become a range of forbidding hills heavily covered in native bush.

"There's a whole lot of families in the same boat," the woman went on. "There's farms all along that twenty-five mile stretch of coast. Got a cousin on one m'self." She ran her hand through her hair in a harassed gesture. "Oh, well, I'd better get back to the kitchen and have a look at the dinner. The gong goes at quarter past six, after the bar's empty. Dining-room is

26

off the hall downstairs. First door to the right."

She would have left the room at this point, if Sharon had not called her back. "But how do I catch this . . . this boat?"

"Leaves in the morning from the jetty at the end of the road. Did you notice the sea when you got here?"

"Yes."

"Well, Nick Kane takes his launch along the coast four days a week. Leaves here about eight and gets back about four. Stops at the bays and drops off the papers, milk and groceries. And he'll take passengers too."

"Where can I find him?"

"Right in the pub. He lives here." She nodded down the corridor. "Number fourteen. That's his room. He's a permanent."

She lumbered off down the passage towards the stairs and Sharon went back into the bedroom to stand by the window and contemplate the unfamiliar scenery. Somewhere behind those inaccessible hills was Brent, quite unaware that the girl with whom he had enjoyed a mild flirtation was only ten miles away.

But she quickly corrected herself. It was not a mild flirtation. It had been real.

She felt hot and dirty after the long journey. It had taken part of the night in the rail-car and part of this day in a train to get to where she could catch the bus which only came to Te Kiri in the evenings. She had slept fitfully on the rail car and was desperately tired so that the single bed looked inviting, but she knew that should she succumb to the need for rest she would probably not sleep. There were too many things to think about and too many things to do. She was a person who enjoyed wonderful health and could not stay depressed for long. Even the lack of sleep could not dim the sparkle in her eyes or the youth and verve of her step.

Along the passage she found a bathroom with, miraculously it seemed, plenty of boiling hot water and, after a bath, she felt better but ravenously hungry and, while she combed her hair in the bedroom, she waited impatiently for the dinner gong.

Apparently the bar was just beneath her bedroom and the noise penetrated the floorboards, but, soon after six it began to lessen and at a quarter past, as the woman had predicted, the gong sounded loudly.

She was the first person into the dining-room. She was surprised to see that there were six tables laid for dinner and decided that the permanent boarders must be many more than the woman had led her to believe. She waited uncertainly, not knowing whether to sit down at the nearest table or wait to be shown where to sit.

After a while the woman who had shown her to her room, put her head around the door that appeared to lead to the kitchen.

"Ah, you are here. Thought you might be hungry."

Sharon was getting used to the woman's odd manner by now and only replied, "Yes. Can I have dinner now please?"

"Mmm. Just sit where you like. Mrs. Marvell's supposed to do the waiting. She's the boss's wife. Don't know where she is. Usually sleeps in the afternoons. She'll be down in a minute I guess."

"Do I have to wait?"

"No. I'll fix you up. What'll you have? Hoggett or beef?"

"Beef, please."

The head disappeared and she sat down

at a table under a window that looked out on a dry, baked yard.

An elderly man came in, looked rather startled to see her there, and sat down at a table. The woman came back bearing a plate. Sharon was grateful to see that it was well filled with meat and vegetables. She was so hungry she hardly noticed the man who entered the dining-room just then. It was only when she heard the woman saying, "Ah, Nick, this lady wants to see you," that she looked up and found herself being observed by Nick Kane.

He was so dark that subconsciously she knew he was partly Maori in origin, though she did not give it a conscious thought. She had rather expected him to be a weather-beaten sailor and middle-aged and she was temporarily disconcerted to find him to be no more than thirty, with strong clearly drawn features. He was wearing an open-necked shirt and light-coloured summer slacks and he looked clean and cool and healthy.

His two hands held the back of a chair lightly. He smiled slightly; a friendly, disarming smile.

"What can I do for you?"

"I want to get to the Warden's farm. I believe you take a boat out there."

"Uhuh."

"Do you have room for me?"

"I guess so. Be at the jetty at eight in the morning. You know where that is?"

"Well, no. I've never been in Te Kiri before."

"Did you see the sea at the end of the road?"

"Yes."

"The road leads to Te Kiri bay. Just go down to the beach. You can't miss the jetty. The boat's anchored alongside. Name's on the side. She's called the *Louise*."

"I'll be there at eight. How long does it take to get out to . . . to . . . what is the place called?"

"Warden's Cove. About an hour and a half if the wind's right."

The woman from the kitchen interrupted them. "What'll you have? Hoggett as usual?" she asked Nick and he was forced to give her his attention and return to his table.

After dinner, though she was tired, it was

31

still too hot and too early for bed and Sharon wandered out through the front door into the cooler evening air and settled down on one of the wooden forms, studying the range of hills again and thinking about Brent Warden. Though it was after seven o'clock, the bar was slowly filling up again and the street resounded with the sound of male voices raised in song. Through the open window she could see the men in their shirt sleeves leaning on the bar and in the background Nick Kane was quietly strumming a guitar. Attracted by his quiet strength, his unconscious air of confidence in himself, she observed him thoughtfully. His long brown fingers easily found the chords on the strings. He played with his head lowered giving all his attention to the sound of the guitar. Now and then, above the indifferent voices of the men in the bar, he harmonized in a fine baritone.

The music stopped, the men pushed forward to refill their glasses, and, looking up from his instrument, he caught her watching him. He smiled briefly. She looked away disconcerted.

But she was composed again when he came outside to join her on the veranda.

"Why don't you come inside?" he asked.

"Into the bar?"

"Mmm."

She was just a little shocked by the suggestion. A bar was a place that she had been led to believe was out-of-bounds for women, for ladies anyway.

"I've never been in a bar in my life."

"But it's different in a place this size. Not like the cities . . ."

"I suppose so."

"The music will probably go on all night." There was a slight husky sound to his voice that suggested that singing was his natural means of communication.

"I enjoyed the music," she offered. "You have a very nice voice."

He shrugged. "Thanks. Why not come inside and join in?"

"All right. Why not?"

He waited for her to precede him into the hall and through the door to the bar. Of the twenty or so men inside only one or two turned to look at her. She was relieved to see the woman from the kitchen and another woman whom she took to be the proprietor's wife were also there.

"What would you like to drink?" Nick Kane asked her.

"Could I have a small sherry? That's all I ever have. Just sometimes."

He grinned. "Of course."

She stood, holding the glass, not really wanting to drink the contents, quite happily observing the men and sprinkling of women in the bar all relaxed and apparently enjoying themselves. One or two of the group were intent on a game of darts and, furthest away from Sharon, a group persisted in singing in faulty harmony.

"Here, Nick, play that damned thing," one of them shouted suddenly, and, unself-consciously, without argument, Nick Kane picked up his guitar and joined in. For a moment she was alone on the fringe of the room, and Sharon found herself confronted by the woman from the kitchen.

"You get jacked up for Nick to take you out tomorrow morning?" the woman asked amiably.

"Yes, thank you."

"The Wardens know you're coming?"

34

"Oh . . . No. I'm going to surprise them." Sharon wished the woman would go away and stop quizzing her.

"Surprise 'em. You'll give them a shock, that's what."

"What do you mean?"

"They don't like visitors, the Wardens. Specially folk just dropping in."

Despite herself and her reluctance to discuss her affairs with anyone Sharon was forced to ask, "Why not?"

"Ah, yes. Why not? I'd like to know that m'self. They keep to themselves, the Wardens do. Ever since young Margaret Warden died. Very suspicious."

"Suspicious?"

"Margaret Warden dying the way she did. You know about that I suppose."

Sharon avoided a direct answer. "How . . . how did she die?"

"Fell from the upstairs veranda of the homestead. Went right through the railing on to the concrete path. Ugh! Awful. Took Judith with her. Very sad that."

"Judith?"

"Didn't they tell you about Judith?"

"Tell me? Oh, no. I haven't seen them for some time. Several years."

"That poor girl has been in a wheelchair ever since. Injured her back in the fall. And only—what is she?—twenty-three?"

"You mean they both fell off the veranda?" Sharon asked, ignoring the question.

"Mmm. Judith saw her fall and tried to stop her. She got pulled down too. Seems she landed on top of Mrs. Warden and that cushioned her fall a bit."

"How dreadful." Sharon stared across the room, appalled. What a terrible thing to have happened to Brent's wife. No wonder he acted strangely at times.

"When was this?" she asked her willing informant.

"Oooh . . . about a year ago. Poor Judith's only just come out of the hospital."

How could anyone, a responsible adult, fall from a balcony accidentally? Sharon wondered, and, as though she had spoken aloud, the woman went on, "It was a funny business and the police were out there for weeks. It got quite exciting here for a while, always cops in the pub. Big detective men from Auckland, those sort. But Mrs. Warden used to take turns. She

36

was an . . . epileptic . . . and it seems she took a turn on the veranda and fell against the railing. It was about eighty years old and rotted. However it seems no one had noticed that the railing was full of borer."

Oh, Brent, Brent. Sharon's brain was full of urgent, thrusting questions, but her pride would not let her question the woman further. This was Brent's affair and he must tell her himself. She was glad that at that moment Nick drew nearer and put the guitar back on a seat along the wall.

"Wouldn't you like to sit down?" he asked her.

"No, no thank you. I think I'll go to bed. I know it's early but I've come a long way today and I've got to be on the beach at eight o'clock. Remember?"

"I'll wait for you."

She smiled widely, her eyes sparkling.

"Good night. See you in the morning."

But she found it difficult to sleep despite her tiring day. She went over and over in her mind the events the woman from the kitchen had described. And who is Judith? she asked herself. *Who* is Judith?

4

TE KIRI was already soaking up the sun when Sharon left the hotel the next morning and made her way down the main street towards the triangle of blue sea. She emerged from the patch of scrub and toi toi that lined the edge of the path where it met the beach, on to a long strip of wide, sweeping sand. Though she was preoccupied with thoughts of Brent and what she had learned of him, her breath was taken away by the beauty of the scene before her; the layers of milky-blue sky, turquoise sea and almost yellow sand. A wooden jetty—none too safe in appearance—jutted out into the blue expanse of sea, and the beach and the water just beyond the lacey breakers were cluttered with small boats.

She was wearing slim-fitting slacks and a white blouse with a large face-framing sun hat and carrying only a small tote bag with what she thought she would need for the day inside. Her other belongings she had left in her room at the hotel where the proprietor was expecting her back for dinner that evening. Just what she could expect of the day she did not know. What would Brent do when she suddenly appeared on his doorstep? Could she hope to be invited to stay? Perhaps it would have been better to have sent him a note and asked him to meet her in Te Kiri. Until now she had not thought beyond finding Brent. Should she go back and just write him a note? But she brushed this thought away and her direct, independent nature asserted itself. Brent had taken the initiative and led her to believe he loved her and she would make him face the situation squarely so that at least she knew why she had been dropped so casually. No false pride or a natural reticence at approaching Brent in his own home would deter her.

She made her way along the jetty, feeling the bright sun warm on her bare arms, and there ahead was the *Louise*, gently rising and falling as the breakers foamed in and out. The boat was something like twenty-four feet long with a natural-wood cabin and bright, white paint. It looked well-cared for and clean. She waved gaily as she saw Nick Kane aboard apparently stowing away parcels and mail for the trip.

He grinned back and helped her into the cockpit and she openly admired his boat.

"What a honey," she said. "How long have you had her?"

"Two years. I bought the run off the man who owned her and the boat went with it."

"May I looked inside?"

"Sure." He pushed the door open for her and she entered the neat, little cabin. She thought it was wonderful and her pleasure in it showed on her mobile face. There were two bunks, a galley at the far end with a two-burner spirit stove and a large cupboard underneath, and a set of table and chairs. The stained-wood walls were dotted with pictures of ships and there were some that Sharon, even as inexperienced as she was in these matters, recognized.

"And do you ever stay at sea all night and sleep here?" she asked with vivid interest.

"Quite often. If the weather gets too

rough while I'm doing a run I put in at one of the bays for the night. And sometimes I stay out all night just because—" He shrugged. "Because I prefer the sea to land perhaps."

"What a wonderful way to live."

Completely at ease they held each other's attention for a moment. Nick moved and looked at his watch. "Time to cast off. Eight o'clock."

"Am I the only passenger today then?" she asked following him and watching while he released the boat from the jetty.

"Uhuh."

He was in the cockpit concentrating on steering the boat away from her moorings. The engine chugged dutifully and the distance to the jetty widened.

"How long did you say it will take to get to . . . to Warden's Cove?"

He turned the wheel carefully. "About an hour and a half."

She sat down on one of the seats that lined the cockpit, not knowing what an attractive picture she made against the sunny blue of the sky and sea. Her face and bare arms were brown with the summer sun for she tanned easily and was naturally olive-skinned.

Gradually the boat chugged around the headland and new vistas came into view, more sheltered bays with good green farm-land that reached almost to the water's edge and behind it a dark mass of bush-clad ranges. Each bay had its own home-stead: large, old wooden buildings nestling in their cultivated gardens. Sometimes a shepherd's cottage graced the rolling country and always there were woolsheds and stock-yards. Each bay had its own small jetty and was decorated with a number of small boats. Then more sheer cliffs until the next bay.

Sharon watched the scenery with interest. This was all new to her and she wondered about the people who lived on these farms, hemmed in by water and land, isolated in their own little communities.

"What do the children do for schooling?" she asked with interest.

He was studying her face though she did not realize it and, as she turned to ask the question, he turned quickly back to the wheel. "Mostly they take correspondent lessons. Then, when they get to high school age, they go away to boarding schools."

"Do . . . do the Wardens have any children?" she asked, not looking at him.

"Uhuh. A boy about eleven. Danny Warden." He looked at her speculatively. "You don't know the family?"

She realized that it must seem odd to him to have her going to call on the Wardens when she did not even know that Brent had a son.

"No. Not the family. Just Brent Warden. I . . . I met him once casually and he invited me to call on them if I ever came up this way."

She flushed a little at the lie. She was too direct a person to enjoy lying—even if the lie was a small one. And somehow she did not like lying to him.

"You seem to have picked the wrong time. Brent Warden has been away for a few weeks. He hasn't got back yet."

"Oh." She was taken by surprise. Somehow she had felt sure that Brent would have come straight home when he had deserted her. It had not occurred to

43

her that he might continue his holiday. She was silent with dismay.

"Does that alter things a bit?" He was watching her closely.

"I expected to find him at home. It's my own fault. I should have made some inquiries first . . . or . . . rung up or something . . ."

"You weren't to know . . ."

"No."

They were silent for a while. In the pit of her stomach the fluttering that meant she was going to see him subsided. She relaxed a little, not realizing until that moment how taut she had been.

"No doubt his family will be glad to meet you," he offered.

"Oh, well, it's too late now. I can't ask you to take me back. I'll just see whoever is at home." Perhaps after all it might be for the best.

"He'll probably get back in a day or two. It was all over Te Kiri that he'd gone for a month. People in Te Kiri like to keep these things straight; keep their fingers on the pulse of things. And there's been plenty of talk about the Wardens."

"Because of Mrs. Warden's death?"

"And other things. I shouldn't be saying this to you, but if you go there not knowing the family you're in for a bit of a shock."

"I gather so. Everybody seems to warn me . . . The waitress at the hotel made it her business to tell me a few things."

"What sort of things?"

"About Brent's wife's death for one thing. Such a dreadful tragedy."

"Yes."

"And she said someone called Dorothy Warden is—how did she put it?—an odd one."

"That's Brent's aunt. His father's sister. I guess the townspeople might call her odd. For one thing she never goes into town. No one has seen much of her at all. She just stays on the farm. Te Kiri people are always suspicious of people who don't mix. You'll see her waiting at Warden's Cove probably. She's a thin woman with fly-away grey hair standing up all around her head. She does have a strange look in her eye—well, lately anyway. But she seems harmless enough. She comes down to their jetty to get the supplies some days. I get along with her all right. Just talk to her about gardening and you'll make out. She does nearly all the gardening around the place, crazy about flowers." He pointed to a tray of plants among the parcels. "Those are for her. I'm always bringing plants in . . ."

"She's Brent's aunt you said?"

"Mmm. She's never married and always lived at the homestead. It belonged to Brent's father and Brent is the oldest son. He inherited it when the old man died. Cole took it badly when he didn't get part of it, but old Mr. Warden provided for him financially and he couldn't upset the will. He does most of the work around the place. He's a farmer at heart, Cole is. Brent isn't." For a moment Sharon thought she could detect a faint sarcasm in his voice. "He's a gentleman. He's got a lot of money invested in stocks and shares I believe. Doesn't need the farm. Cole runs the place with the help of a shepherd. There's a lot of it. Several thousand acres. Cole needs more help but it's hard to get labour to live out here. They have some seasonal help and sometimes they manage to get workers who'll live there for a while. It's about the best farm round here. The shepherd's a bit . . . well, different, too. He served ten years for murdering his wife. Ten years doesn't seem much, does it? The court apparently thought there was some provocation. There was another man involved. When he got out and came back to the district, no one wanted to take him on. But Cole met him in the bar at the pub one afternoon and gave him a job. When Margaret Warden died he was the first one the police checked on."

"But why? I mean she fell, didn't she? There wasn't any question of . . . of murder?"

"They came to the conclusion that she'd fallen."

"You don't think she did?"

The blue sea was calm. The boat churned up only the faintest white spray. She stood up and looked over the side. "You don't think she did?" she asked again.

"I don't think anything about it at all," he answered slowly and deliberately. "But there was a lot of talk just before it happened about Brent and Judith. Judith was Margaret's sister."

"But she fell off the balcony too."

"Yes."

She watched the sea, feeling his reluctance to discuss the matter further. He didn't want to tell her about it, but he was suspicious. But there was something she had to know.

"You mean Brent and Judith were . . . were in love?"

"So it seemed."

"But they haven't married since."

"No." He paused. "But Judith is in a wheelchair now. Things are . . . are rather different."

She was shocked into indignation. "You mean you think that because she can't walk Brent would . . ."

"Don't get all het up about it," he silenced her, grinning slightly. "You asked me. I didn't want to discuss Brent Warden with you."

She leaned over the rail and watched the foaming white sea, unaware that he watched her oddly, wondering where she fitted in Brent Warden's life and what he meant to her.

For a long time she watched the snug farms with their outbuildings and backdrops of bush wishing that she was an

48

artist who could transfer the scenes to canvas. After a while he disappeared into the cabin and she was momentarily alarmed.

"Is it all right to leave the wheel like that?" she asked looking through the door and seeing him absorbed at the bench.

"Uhuh. It'll just keep going steadily in this direction. I'm making some coffee. Like a cup?"

"Yes. Yes, thank you. I would."

She sat down again in the cockpit feeling the slight breeze on her face, despite her mission, enjoying herself. The sea and the open air appealed immensely to her. Soon he emerged from the cabin with a tray containing two cups of coffee and a plate of sandwiches.

"I hope I'm not eating your lunch," she said as she took a sandwich and a cup of coffee. "Do you always feed your passengers?"

"Usually. There's not often more than one at a time. I bring the sandwiches with me, but there's plenty of food in the galley for lunch. The waitress at the pub makes the sandwiches for me in the morning."

"I'm just ready for them," she said.

"The sea air must be making me hungry. It's not two hours since I had breakfast."

He looked at his watch. "Not much further to Warden's Cove. I put in at the next bay to unload some parcels and the one after that's Warden's."

Within half an hour or so she had her first glimpse of Brent's home and it jolted her considerably. A beige-coloured sandy beach outlined the curve of the bay, and, like all the other coves they had passed, a small jetty jutted out to sea. Sheep grazed almost to the water's edge on the gently-rolling green slopes. Some beautiful, tall trees sheltered the woolshed and the shepherd's cottage. But it was the homestead itself that held her attention. It rose from a flat plateau some distance inland; an imposing triple-storeyed wooden structure with decorative turrets and gabled roofs. Just the house that an early pioneer of humble origin might have built for himself in the new country; an imitation of the grand homes he remembered in England.

As the boat chugged in towards the shore she became aware of a group of figures standing on the jetty. The tall, angular figure of a middle-aged woman and the slim figure of a tow-haired boy, the sculptured, still shape of an Alsatian dog.

"That's Miss Warden and Danny waiting for us," Nick told her as though he anticipated a question.

The boat drew nearer and nearer and the two people on the wharf began to take on life-sized proportions. The woman was standing with her head thrown back and soon Sharon could see her features clearly. She was wearing a large, face-framing hat over greying brown hair. Her face was small and her features delicate. Her eyes were wide and vacant in their gaze which gave her the appearance of an adult child. The boy was burnt brown by the sun as though he lived in the open air, his hair bleached almost to white. His features were fine and sensitive, at odds with his outdoor appearance. Even as they approached, Sharon found herself looking for a resemblance to Brent. There was something about the straight body, the set of the head that reminded her of him, but she decided that he must be more like his dead mother.

The two were waiting impatiently yet immobile. As they drew nearer Nick saluted them nonchalantly and they waved briefly back.

Sharon stayed in the cockpit and waited while Nick tied the boat to the jetty. Aunt Dorothy hovered over him.

"I'm hoping you've brought my seedlings," she called out coyly, holding the picture hat on her head, appearing quaint and old-fashioned with her too-long skirt blowing around her legs and somehow reminiscent of a painting by Gainsborough.

Nick began to lift the tray of plants and the boy hopped into the boat to help him. He glanced warily at Sharon. She smiled quickly, a slight dimple appearing briefly in her cheek.

"Hi," she murmured.

"Hi."

"These will keep you busy," Nick said to the woman as he laid the box on the jetty next to a carton of groceries and a mail bag. She knelt down beside them inspecting their delicate leaves.

"I hope you've been very careful with them. They're not crushed or anything."

"Sure I've been careful."

"They don't look very strong, do they? One has to be so careful when buying from advertisements."

Nick held out his hand and helped Sharon on to the jetty. "I've brought you a visitor," he told the woman and the boy. The dog moved abruptly as though a statue had suddenly been granted life.

The woman stood up slowly, adjusting her hat and the flowing skirt.

"Oh . . ." She was disconcerted by Sharon's presence, and Sharon hastened to explain.

"You won't know me, Miss Warden. I'm Sharon Denholm. I'm a friend of Brent's . . . We met a few weeks ago. He told me to . . . to call if I ever got up this way . . ." She faltered. "I'm on my annual leave and I was passing within twenty miles of here and I'd never seen this place so I thought I'd just come out and say hello to Brent."

The dog moved closer to Sharon, sniffing. She stood absolutely still and made no involuntary movement. She liked animals and knew no fear of them, though this animal was more than half as high as she herself.

The boy said, "Butch, come here," in a warning manner as Sharon put a tentative hand on the dog's head. Without any more warning, the dog quickly stood upright, his paws fighting for a foothold on the front of her blouse. Immediately Nick was between her and the dog forcing the animal from her, and for the first time she saw something other than relaxed good humour in his face. His eyes were narrow, angry and almost afraid.

"Danny, get this thing away from here."

Danny was already tugging at the dog's collar, pulling the animal in against his bare legs.

"For crying out loud why don't you keep an eye on him? He's too big to be jumping all over people."

"He won't hurt her," Danny protested with something like contempt in his voice.

Sharon brushed her hand against the front of her blouse; it was sticky with mud and something else, and she shuddered with faint disgust. "It doesn't matter. He hasn't done any harm. Don't worry about it." She held the raw edges of a long tear in the blouse together with one hand.

"Oh, dear, this is terrible . . ." Miss Warden fluttered around her. "Are you really all right?" Her long fingers moved up to her throat and away again. "Danny if you can't control that dog any better than that he'll have to be sold or kept tied up . . ."

The boy looked at the ground, his mouth tight, and kept his grip on the dog.

"Oh, please, don't worry about it. I'm perfectly all right," Sharon protested again. "It was my fault. I shouldn't have touched him. He doesn't know me . . ."

"You must come up to the house and clean up," Miss Warden murmured. "Brent is away. I'm afraid he's not back yet. He's been away for several weeks . . . a holiday . . ."

"Oh . . . How stupid of me. I just took it for granted that he would be at home. I should have phoned." She looked helplessly at Nick. "Now, what will I do? What time do you go back to Te Kiri?"

"I get back here about two-thirty . . ."

"But you can't think of leaving here like

this," Dorothy Warden interrupted. "I insist that you come up to the house . . ."

"Wouldn't that be inconvenient for you?"

Dorothy Warden smiled fleetingly, uncertainly. She does not want me to stay, Sharon thought. She acts as though she is afraid of something.

"Not at all. I wouldn't dream of letting you go in that state after that awful dog . . ."

Sharon turned to Nick. "Then would you mind stopping for me on the way back?"

"Uhuh." He looked at her seriously. "Are you sure you're all right?"

She flashed him a smile. "Of course."

As though to show Danny that his anger had abated, he ruffled the boy's hair. "Keep an eye on that animal, Danny."

Sharon watched him cast off in the boat almost reluctantly. Compared to these strangers she felt she knew him well. In a lucky accident, the dog had provided her with a good excuse for staying, and yet she had a wild desire to flee this place, to call Nick back, to board the *Louise* and go home. It was almost a premonition. She looked at the homestead and it suddenly became grey and forbidding and mysterious. But the unease was washed away by a fleeting vision of Brent's face. She had come this far and she must go on.

"Can I help carry these things up to the house?" she asked indicating the small pile of goods on the jetty.

"Goodness no! Cole will collect them. I'll just take the mail bag."

"I'll carry it, Aunt Dorothy," Danny offered and slung it over his shoulder. It was small but bulky as though it contained a parcel or two. He started off across the beach ahead of them, following a track through the paddocks towards the homestead. He waited at each gate for them and politely closed them when they were through. The dog followed him obediently, subdued again.

The acre garden of the homestead was surrounded by a waist-high brick wall well over-grown by an ice plant and with a closed iron gate. Inside the wall, flowers, bushes, trees seemed to grow in unplanned profusion, but Sharon knew enough about gardening to realize that only a master hand could create this effect and that someone must be spending hours of work on the garden. As Danny opened the gate, she asked, "Who does all this?"

"The garden?" Dorothy Warden looked surprised. "Why, me. I'm the only one fond of gardening around here, and we just can't get a gardener to live on the place—we're too isolated. Married people like a school handy and single men like to live in the towns where they can . . ." She shrugged. "Well, meet girls . . ."

"It's just beautiful," Sharon enthused sincerely and did not see the pleasure in Dorothy Warden's face. "We only have a small garden at home and I do most of it, but this is what I dream about. A real old-fashioned garden. You are certainly to be congratulated on it."

"Thank you." Dorothy Warden was suddenly demure. She looked away. "I love it of course. It is my whole life . . . and my family of course . . ."

Over the crest of a nearby hill two men appeared on horseback. The pensive mood of Dorothy Warden vanished. She started forward and waved one hand high above her head. "Oohoo. Cole . . ."

The riders came towards them. They

were both young, one a blond boy in his early twenties rather like Danny in appearance, the other small and dark and perhaps ten years older. They both wore dark-coloured jeans and sweat shirts and the blond boy had a handkerchief knotted about his neck. They drew up beside Dorothy; Cole, as Sharon took him to be, a little in front, the dark rider hovering in the background. Their faces were deadly serious, they observed her briefly through narrowed lids.

"The boat has been in, Cole," Dorothy was explaining. "And there's a carton of groceries on the jetty and a tray of asters. Will you bring them up to the house, please?"

"Okay." There was a nasal twang in his voice and, despite the hard exterior, Sharon felt inclined to be amused by him. "Is that all?"

He lifted his head and stared straight at her and Dorothy obviously felt obliged to make an introduction.

"This is Miss . . ."

"Sharon Denholm," Sharon supplied.

"Yes, Miss Denholm. She is a friend of Brent's and just called in . . ."

Cole raised his hand in an ironic salute. "I don't recall Brent ever mentioning her."

"We only met a . . . a short time ago." She had been about to say "a few days ago" but checked herself. Could it really be only a few days ago that she had seen him last?

Cole gestured to his companion to come forward. "This is Hank."

Sharon smiled again. "Hello . . . Hank."

"Howdy."

Sharon kept a straight face with difficulty and when they had moved off with Dorothy still begging them to be very careful with the plants, she could not resist saying, "They're . . . different, aren't they? I mean . . . their voices . . . Are they Americans?"

Dorothy laughed, a high, silvery laugh. "Goodness me, no! Cole is Brent's brother, a born and bred New Zealander. He's just imitating the actors in the wild west pictures. You know the ones I mean. He's always been crazy about the wild west ever since he was a boy. Likes to think he's a cowboy and that this place is a ranch." The high laugh again. "Imagine. Warden's Cove a ranch! He sleeps out in the cottage with Hank. He calls it the bunkhouse and the place is full of wild west novels and comics, and pictures, and records by singers with horrible accents. Hank just worships Cole—yes, just worships him—and he goes along with it all. He's much older in the head than Cole, but he humours him."

"Hank. Is that his real name?"

"Dear me, no. It's Henry. Cole changed it to Hank. It sounds right you see. Cole's real name is Arthur. He was called after Brent's father. He started calling himself Cole as a little boy. He just wouldn't answer to anything else."

Sharon listened with interest. These were the people Brent knew, amongst whom he lived and they were important to her. She looked for Danny but he had gone towards the house with the mail bag and the dog.

"And the little boy?" she asked. "He is Brent's son?"

"Oh dear, of course. I should have introduced him, but that awful dog confused me."

Dorothy shut the gate behind them and they went on between the lawns, along the winding, neatly-trimmed path towards the house. The trees cleared a little and there was the homestead towering over them, massive, almost bizarre in its ornamental architecture. Despite herself, Sharon looked up. There across the front of the top storey was the balcony. Her eyes travelled downwards to the concrete path at their feet, bordered by lawns and flower-beds, and she could see in her mind the body of Brent's wife and the crippled form of his sister-in-law lying there waiting to be found. In that single event she felt sure lay the answer to her quest, the explanation.

"What are you looking at?" Dorothy Warden asked sharply.

Sharon turned towards her. Dorothy's eyes were wide and frightened, wary.

"Only the garden," Sharon lied quickly. She could not lie easily and it showed on her face. Dorothy turned away.

"Let's go inside," she murmured, "and get you cleaned up."

She led the way up the steps on to an ornate veranda and through an open pair

62

of double doors into a wide vestibule. Sharon looked about her with interest. From either side more wide doors, through which she could see, opened on to huge rooms, one furnished as a dining-room and one as a lounge in heavy antique furniture. Further back another door opened on to a hall at the back of the house. Ahead a flight of stairs with a solid black banister disappeared up on to another floor. In the shadowy corner beneath the stairs she was startled to see what appeared to be the large figure of a man, but, as her eyes became used to the gloom, she saw that it was in reality a complete suit of armour standing there.

"Is that you, Aunt Dorothy?" The quiet voice came from the sitting-room.

"Yes, dear, it's me." Dorothy went across to the door. "You're in here." She turned back to Sharon. "Come and meet my niece, Judith."

Sharon moved towards the voice. Judith! The woman whom Brent had loved—or so it was said. She followed Dorothy into the lounge.

She was sitting in a wheelchair across the room in front of a latticed bay-window.

As they entered she turned the wheel-chair towards them and Sharon could see her clearly. She was young, no older than Sharon; her figure in the chair was slight and she held herself very straight. Her frock was also young with a small soft collar and wide skirt that finished just at her knees so that two long, brown legs were exposed. The frock had no sleeves and her arms were brown and nicely-shaped. For a moment Sharon could not absorb the picture properly. She had expected Judith to—well, look crippled, she told herself. But, other than the wheel-chair, nothing suggested it. She looked like any very-attractive young girl sitting rather carefully in a chair. The light from the window showed blue tints in the jet-black hair that was caught in a french roll at the back of her head. In contrast her skin was surprisingly pale; her eyes were wide and blue. Despite a desire to dislike her for what she had apparently been to Brent—perhaps still was—Sharon could not miss the sweetness, the gentleness of her expression.

"I've brought you a visitor," Dorothy explained. "This is Miss Denholm. She just came in with Nick's boat. She came to see Brent. I told her he's away at the moment, but that terrible dog of Danny's messed her up. Just stood right up and pawed her, such a shock for her. Of course I insisted on her staying until Nick gets back this afternoon."

"Of course." Judith smiled a quiet welcome. "I'm so sorry you had such an unpleasant experience with our dog. You must let me lend you some clean clothes. We look about the same size."

"That's very kind of you." Sharon studied her carefully trying to get beneath the surface. Surely Judith must be suspicious of her association with Brent?

"Is there anything you want, dear?" Dorothy fussed about her.

"No, thank you. I was just listening to the radio and looking at the garden. Perhaps we might have lunch outside do you think?"

"If you'd like to. I'll attend to it as soon as I've found Miss Denholm some clean clothes."

"Look in my room for something to fit her." Surely she must wonder how Brent and this strange girl had met?

Dorothy led Sharon back into the vestibule and up two flights of stairs to the third storey. From the landing there was a long corridor each side with several bedrooms opening from it. They went into the one that was Judith's, and, while Dorothy was hunting in the wardrobe, Sharon studied the room with interest. It was panelled and high-ceilinged with glass doors opening on to a balcony that seemed to overlook the front garden. Perhaps the balcony where it had happened? There was a three-quarter bed with a quilted spread that matched the curtains, a heavy old-fashioned wardrobe and a beautiful Queen Anne dressing-table.

Dorothy turned round holding a blue linen frock in her hand. "This should fit you." She looked at Sharon speculatively. "When Judith stands up she's just about your height."

"She can stand up?"

"She can move about a little with the aid of hand crutches. She just has no power of movement in her legs." A distant, watching look came into her eyes. "You know about . . . about her accident?"

Dorothy would think Brent had told her, but Sharon murmured, "Of course."

"Such a brave, brave thing she did."

"Yes."

"And she has been so brave since. Not a word of complaint that she has lost so much. She's twenty-two and her whole life was still ahead of her. Now . . ." She shrugged. "She is so good and patient and she does all she can to help me with the house, the vegetables, the sewing. She can make her own bed and dust about a bit. It's very hard to get anyone to live out here and help with the work and this is such a big house. I manage as best I can and what I can't get done in a day just gets left. I like to spend so much time in the garden. In the afternoons we usually move outdoors in the nice weather and Judith knits or does the mending while I weed the borders. She's a very sweet girl. Not really my niece you know, but I feel as if she is. Her mother and father were already dead when Brent married her sister and she just moved in with us. Brent just insisted. Oh, it breaks my heart to see her as she is . . ."

Tears flooded her eyes for a moment and

Sharon was moved to sympathy. Obviously Dorothy Warden loved Judith. And who could help it, Sharon wondered. Brent?

She found she was beginning to like Dorothy Warden despite her fluttering rather over-anxious manner. She liked her air of innocence and the kindly way she talked about Judith, the way she apparently shouldered the burden of running this enormous house and garden. But she could not quite understand her. The frightened, wary look that came and went unexpectedly, the way she suddenly became still, her head held slightly on one side, quiet, as though she was listening for something. She did it often and Sharon found that she too was listening. But for what? For Judith to call perhaps?

In a bathroom adjoining Judith's bedroom she washed and changed into the blue linen frock. Afterwards she made her way down the stairs, and, as though she waited for her footsteps, Dorothy appeared in the entrance hall from the direction of the kitchen.

"I'm just putting the lunch on," she said. "Are you more comfortable now?"

"Yes, thank you very much."

"Judith is in the garden. Would you like to join her while I'm busy?"

"Can't I help you with the lunch? Please, do let me."

"Of course not. Everything's under control. Come and sit with Judith."

5

PART of the garden at the back of the house had been paved in a large brick square which was sheltered by an enormous old oak tree. A wicker table, several chairs and a couch suggested that eating outside was a habit in the household. Judith was sitting in the shade on the brick patio in her wheelchair apparently engrossed in a book. For a moment she did not hear Sharon approach and Sharon studied her quietly. What is she really like under that sweet exterior? she wondered. And how could Brent resist her, even crippled as she was?

Judith looked up and—did Sharon imagine it, or was there just a slight hesitation?—before she smiled quietly.

"Do come and sit down."

"Thank you." Sharon sat carefully in one of the wicker chairs. "And thank you for lending me this frock. I've rinsed the blouse out. It might dry in time for me to catch the boat back perhaps."

"It doesn't matter whether it does or not. You can return the frock some other time."

"That's very nice of you." She looked around at the garden. "How lovely this all is."

"Yes." Sharon turned as Judith spoke and found Judith watching her seriously, intently. "How long have you known Brent?" she asked.

"Just a few weeks." Sharon was on the defensive.

"You met him while he has been away?"

"Yes."

Judith turned away and Sharon could see her face only in profile; such a fragile, exquisite profile, but the set of the mouth, the remote haunted expression in the eyes betrayed an emotion Judith fought to control. With a woman's quick intuition about such things Sharon told herself, so she loves him, she really loves Brent.

They were interrupted by Dorothy Warden who came out to set the table and soon Danny appeared with the dog loping behind him and demanded, "What's for lunch? I'm starving."

"It's cold lamb and salad. Now go and wash your hands," Dorothy told him.

"They're clean. I haven't been doing anything."

"No? You've been playing with that dog all morning."

He went reluctantly into the house while Sharon insisted on helping Dorothy to set the table.

"There will be six of us," Dorothy told her. "Cole and Hank will be over." The corners of her mouth turned up slightly as she used their names as if they amused her.

She had hardly spoken when the two horsemen came round the side of the house on foot, walking with an exaggerated swagger, their thumbs looped over the edge of the pockets in their jeans.

"Waal," Cole drawled. "What's t' eat?"

"It'll be ready in a minute," Dorothy answered disappearing into the house.

The two men stretched their legs out and relaxed in two of the wicker chairs while Sharon helped Dorothy with the lunch. As she moved around the table setting out the knives and forks, they watched her through half-closed eyes.

"And where do you come from? What part of the country?" Cole drawled.

"A long way off. Hawkes Bay."

"Waal . . . Brent sure gets around. He's a tiger for the women is our Brent."

Sharon could feel the hot colour rising in her face and she looked pointedly away.

"Stop that, Cole," Judith silenced him quickly. "You are embarrassing Miss Denholm." Her luminous eyes studied Sharon. "Ignore him, please. He behaves stupidly at times. He's not fully grown."

This little bit of sarcasm did not seem to annoy Cole. He kept calm and unruffled. "Oh, well, the lord and master will be home in the morning."

Judith's fingers gripped the arms of her chair, her face became tense. Sharon paused behind the table and waited. Aunt Dorothy came into the garden from the house just at that moment and exclaimed, "In the morning? Why, Cole, how do you know?"

He was in no hurry to answer but surveyed them nonchalantly. "Te Kiri rang up this morning," he said at last. "There's a telegram at the Post Office."

Judith relaxed in her chair, her hands in her lap, but Sharon could see that she was not composed. She was breathing heavily and her bottom lip trembled. She really loves him terribly, she thought.

"Why didn't you tell us earlier?" she asked Cole, quietly.

"I didn't see no need."

"Well," Dorothy chattered, "isn't that nice? He's coming home at last."

"I thought that would make you all happy," Cole murmured. "Brent's coming home and everybody will be happy." His eyes moved around the little group. "'Cept Hank and me, of course."

"Cole," Judith said sharply, but he was not to be stopped.

"The little god will come home and take over. But who will do all the work around the place? Hank and me, that's who. Like we always do. Brent's a gentleman." His voice dripped sarcasm. "He just runs around having a lovely time with all the ladies." He bowed his head mockingly towards Judith and Sharon. "But who runs this ranch? Me. I run it with Hank here."

Aunt Dorothy tried to pour oil on

troubled waters. "We know you do, Cole. You work very hard and we all appreciate it, and Hank works hard too . . ."

"Sure, sure . . . Hank works hard. I work hard." He suddenly sat up straight. "But who makes all the dough? Brent, that's who. The little tin god."

Judith's voice was icy. "Cole, if you can't behave like a gentleman when we have a guest, please leave us alone and take your bad manners somewhere else. You are right. Brent is a gentleman and he would never make a scene like you have just done."

Cole shrugged and relaxed in the chair, not with remorse, but as though this were familiar ground and he couldn't care less. Irrationally Sharon found herself wanting to protest that Brent had not acted like a gentleman, that he had courted her in a serious fashion and left her without a word. She felt almost sorry for Cole. Despite his boorish manners, would he have been as rude to Sharon and to her parents as Brent had been when he did not arrive to meet them. But she shuddered realizing how much Cole hated his brother.

To help Aunt Dorothy in this difficult situation, she tried to change the subject.

"Do you have a phone out here?" she asked. "I would have thought it was impossible."

Gratefully, Dorothy answered, "Oh, yes, we've had one for quite a while. There's no road but they managed to string a telephone wire across the ranges. We've almost been promised a road the year after next . . ."

So Brent would be home in the morning. Did that mean that she might see him tonight in Te Kiri. Sharon was deep in thought, when Judith said, "Your trip won't be wasted after all, Miss Denholm. I suggest you stay the night and see Brent in the morning."

She wants to witness our meeting, Sharon told herself. She wants to know who I am and what I mean to Brent. And who can blame her?

She protested because she felt it would be expected of her but it was a half-hearted protest. She knew that Judith would insist that she stayed, would offer her the necessary clothes to stay overnight. And what difference did it make? She was going to see Brent and sort out this mess and here was as good as anywhere else.

6

AT half past two that afternoon Sharon excused herself to go down to the beach to wait for Nick Kane's boat to pass on its homeward trip.

"There's no need for you to worry about it," Aunt Dorothy had protested. "Danny will tell Nick. He always goes down when the boat's due." But for some reason she could not explain even to herself, Sharon wanted to go. It would be ungracious to just not appear after he had been kind in the morning, she told herself.

At half past two she and Danny and the dog were on the beach, but there was no sign of the boat. The bay was calm and the towering cliffs sung in a faint heat mist. Something in Sharon that was young and gay despite the urgency of her position made her kick her shoes off and paddle in the gentle waves. The dog bounded up and down the shore and Danny, in bathing trunks, plunged deep into the sea. Soon the three of them collapsed on the beige-coloured sand exhausted in the heat. Feeling young in the company of the boy and the dog exhilarated by the sea and the tangy, fresh air, Sharon stretched her arms above her head and breathed deeply.

"Oh, what a wonderful day and what a wonderful place to live."

She turned to smile at Danny who was lying on the sand on his stomach but found him watching her seriously, a distant look in his eyes.

"When you were paddling in the sea you reminded me of my mother."

Immediately Sharon was serious, sympathetic to his mood and to his loss, and feeling that she was on the brink of a revelation, a clue to Brent's past.

"You mean I am like her?"

"No, but she used to take her shoes off and walk along the beach. We used to have our lunch down here often. We don't do it any more."

"What did she look like? Your mother."

"Like Auntie Judith."

"Of course. They were sisters, weren't they?'

He squirmed over and lay on his back

shielding his eyes against the sun with the back of his hand.

"Mmm. Only Mum was older, a whole lot older. 'Bout ten years."

She ached with sympathy for him. Such a dreadful thing to happen to one's mother. "You must miss her a lot," she ventured.

"Mmm." She could not see his face for the hand.

"It's a year since she . . . died, isn't it?"

"'Bout that." He sat up suddenly and looked her full in the face. "She fell off the balcony one night."

"Yes, I heard that. Was it at night?"

"Mmm." His eyes were remote. "It was awful late, after midnight."

"What was she doing on the balcony after midnight, Danny?"

"She went out to shush Butch."

"To shush Butch?"

"Mmm. He was on the lawn growling at something—must've seen a 'possum probably. He'd been howling for about ten minutes. Auntie Judith and Mum both went out to tell him to be quiet. And I went out too."

"On to the balcony?"

"Nope. I went out of the house on to the lawn. Butch was tied up to his kennel under the trees, to keep him off Aunt Dorothy's garden. He was growling like mad."

"You . . . you saw your mother fall."

"No . . . I was looking at Butch just then . . . I saw her come out on to the balcony, and Auntie Judith . . ." A strange look flitted across his face.

"Yes?" She held her breath, suddenly tense.

"Nothing," he said.

But she would not let the moment pass. There was an urgency about him that suggested he knew something important. "Danny, was there someone else? Was there?"

"Yes."

"Who was it?"

"I don't know. But there was. I could just see someone standing in the doorway, but it was dark. It might have been just a shadow."

They looked at each other full of misgiving. And suddenly the bright afternoon seemed cold, a little chill wind swept across Sharon.

"Was it a man or a woman?"

"I don't know."

"Didn't you tell your father about it? Whoever it was must have seen your mother fall. They could have explained it all to the police . . ." She was talking almost to herself, thinking it over carefully. All she had heard about the night had suggested that no one had witnessed the accident.

"I tried to tell Dad, but he said I was wrong, there wasn't anybody. He said it was too dark to see properly and that if anyone was on the balcony they'd say so. But nobody did . . ."

"And you didn't tell the police?"

"No. I thought Dad was probably right and it was only a shadow . . ."

"And did anyone admit to being on the balcony when the accident happened?"

"No . . ."

They were silent for a moment while Sharon thought it over and Danny remembered.

"You don't really think it was only a shadow, do you Danny?"

He considered this for a moment. "No," he said. Suddenly his face became animated and lost its introspective expression. He pointed out to sea. "Look! Here comes the *Louise*."

Nick's boat had appeared around the nearest point and was chugging into the bay. Danny raced off across the sand towards the jetty though it would take ten minutes for the boat to arrive. Sharon wandered down more slowly thinking over again what Danny had said. She was convinced that there had been another person on the balcony that night and for some reaosn they had not divulged the fact. But perhaps there were things that Danny, as a child, had not heard and did not know, perhaps the person, whoever it was, had told the police. She must not take it for granted that a child of eleven would know all that had happened that night and the weeks and months following. But he had told the truth as he saw it, she was sure. Which meant that Brent had persuaded him not to mention the third person on the balcony to anyone else.

As the boy drew near and she saw the now-familiar figure at the wheel she waved out. Nick waved back. He was hatless and a slight breeze stirred his dark hair, his skin was golden brown in the sun and she thought how attractive he looked.

The boat chugged in.

"Hi," she said, as he sprang easily on to the jetty.

"Hello." He smiled his slow smile and she felt warm and friendly towards him. He was very appealing. She was in love with Brent and, to her, he was the perfect, handsome, intelligent male, but she knew in her heart that he was just slightly aloof, there was something about him, a depth she could not fathom, and it made her feel horribly young and unsophisticated. But though she had known Nick such a short time, she felt at ease with him as though they met on equal terms.

"All set to go?" he asked.

"Well, no, not exactly. I'm staying overnight."

"Oh . . ." He stared thoughtfully at the homestead in the distance. "Is that a good idea?"

This perturbed her and she answered, "That's a funny thing to say. They've had word that Brent will be home tomorrow and Judith insists that I stay to see him. I suppose he'll come in with you in the morning. I'll go back tomorrow afternoon."

He looked about him for Danny who was in the cockpit of the boat, and lowered his voice. "You don't want to get too tangled up with the Wardens, that's all."

"Why not?" She was surprised. It seemed so out of character for him to be interfering in another person's business.

He shrugged. "Forget it. It's none of my business."

But she was not happy as she watched him draw away and finally disappear from sight. She was full of uncertainty. And that night she had cause to remember his words.

She was shown into a bedroom on the top floor, beside Judith's room and over-looking the front of the house. Like Judith's room it was large, comfortable and attractively furnished, and two glass doors opened on to the balcony outside. It was about ten-thirty when they retired to bed. There was quite a routine attached to going to bed she found, and Cole came over from the cottage to carry Judith upstairs. Dorothy Warden explained that they had written to a firm and asked them to put in a lift since the accident but they were still waiting for them to come. Judith, she explained, had one wheelchair upstairs and one down, but it would be a lot easier when the contractors began work on the lift and she could wheel herself in and out and go upstairs on her own.

As soon as Sharon was alone, she stepped out on to the balcony. The garden lay in a quiet darkness and it must have been just such a night that Margaret Warden had fallen from this same balcony. Sharon glanced up and down. There were several sets of lattice doors opening on to it. She went across to the railing and smoothed her hand across it. She drew her hand away sharply as though the rail were hot as she realized that she was standing beside a piece that had obviously been renewed not long since. In the light from her bedroom it gleamed with new cream paint.

"What are you doing?"

She jumped visibly as she heard Judith's voice behind her. From her own room she had wheeled her wheelchair out on to the balcony. Like a guilty child Sharon put both hands behind her and gulped down her fright.

"I'm just getting a breath of fresh air before I turn in. It's so lovely out here . . ."

"Yes. I always come out here for a few minutes before I go to bed." Did she imagine it or was Judith suspicious of her? She was hardly visible in the half-light.

"I'll go to bed now," Sharon murmured. "Can you manage on your own?"

"Oh, yes. I quite easily put myself to bed and get out of it in the mornings. I have two sticks to help me."

But in bed, wearing a pair of Judith's pyjamas, she could not sleep. Was Judith still out on the balcony? But there is nothing sinister about Judith, she told herself. She has one of the sweetest faces I've ever seen. She looks so good, so pure.

She dozed fitfully and was awakened by the sound of a dog growling low in his throat. She turned over and would have gone back to sleep but suddenly became aware of where she was. She lay listening to Butch. What had Danny said? He was tied up on the lawn beside a kennel. After a while she heard Danny's voice, low and urgent. "Be quiet, Butch. Down boy." The dog became silent and the house settled into sleep again.

Again she dozed and when she woke became aware of a shadow across the floor of her room. She lay absolutely still until her eyes grew used to the darkness and she realized that someone was standing on the balcony just outside her wide-open doors. For a moment, she was horribly afraid as if the year-dead Margaret had come back and was waiting in the shadows.

This is ridiculous, she told herself. What's got into me? I don't usually jump at shadows. I haven't often been afraid of anything. Why does this house frighten me? She forced herself to act and got out of bed and pulled on the housecoat that Judith had thoughtfully provided. And as she moved she watched the figure on the balcony. It stood absolutely still facing the garden.

Deliberately she moved across the room and accosted Dorothy Warden. Her head was held slightly on one side in a listening posture and her expression was remote.

"Miss Warden?" Sharon ventured.

"Can you hear it?" the woman asked without moving.

"Hear what?"

"Can't you hear it?"

"You mean the dog?"

"No. Can't you hear it?"

There was a slight movement behind them and Sharon turned sharply. Judith was sitting in her wheelchair, wearing a housecoat, just a few feet away.

"Go back to bed, Aunt Dorothy," she ordered, quietly. "There's nothing to hear. It's just your imagination." Dorothy did not move. "Aunt Dorothy." The voice was just a little sharper and Dorothy turned her head slightly. "Go back to bed. There's nothing here. There isn't anything to hear."

Like a sleep-walker awakening to reality Dorothy blinked and hugged her dressing-gown about her sparse figure as though it were cold.

"How stupid of me," she said. "I should be in bed." Guiltily, stooping a little, she stumbled away.

"I'm sorry if she disturbed you, Miss Denholm," Judith apologized. "She won't wake you up again."

"Please tell me. What was she listening for?"

Judith was silent for a long time. "I don't know," she said at last.

"Was it something to do with the night Mrs. Warden fell off the balcony?"

She expected Judith to be angry, but she remained calm.

"It may be. She does this quite often. We are quite used to it. Something—a noise—wakes her up and she comes out here almost hypnotized—listening for something."

"The dog woke her . . ."

"Perhaps . . ."

"Does anyone else ever hear anything?"

"Of course not. It's all in her own mind."

"But what can it be?"

"I don't know. Perhaps it is something about that night she remembers. Perhaps she hears Margaret screaming . . . I can hear it myself. The scream . . ."

"She screamed?"

"Yes, when she found herself

falling. . . ." She twisted her wheelchair around abruptly. "Good night, Miss Denholm. I'm sorry you've been disturbed."

7

THE boat would be in about nine-thirty and Brent would be on board. From somewhere she must conjure up the nonchalance to face him. It was going to be a disturbing moment when he found her waiting for him in his own home. The thought almost amused her for she was blessed—or was it cursed?—with the ability to laugh at herself. Brent who thought he had cleverly avoided falling permanently into her clutches would arrive at this haven and find her waiting! But she sobered quickly. No, it wasn't like that, she told herself.

"I'm off to meet Dad," Danny shouted as the boat appeared in the distance, and she longed to follow him and see Brent alone on the beach without the watching eyes of Judith and Dorothy, but she could think of no excuse to leave with Danny. And so she waited on the front porch with the other two women for him to come. And, after what seemed an age, he came up the garden path, the dog bounding about his feet, one arm around Danny's shoulders.

He was as immaculate as ever and as attractive. His teeth flashed white as he laughed with Danny, full of good nature, but, as he looked up and saw them waiting on the porch, the laughter died and his expression became remote.

Sharon waited for a shock of surprise when he saw her, but his face registered none. He climbed the steps slowly and dutifully kissed Aunt Dorothy who flung both arms about his neck like an excited child and cried, "Hello, Brent, dear. You've come home at last."

"Hello, Brent," Judith greeted him quietly.

He nodded at her briefly. "How are you?"

He turned to Sharon while Judith replied inaudibly, as though Sharon were a problem which just had to be faced. Which of course, I am, she thought ruefully.

"Hello, Sharon."

Sharon was aware of the other two watching them closely, studying their reaction to each other and she kept calm with difficulty.

"You are not surprised to see me here?"

"No. I had to stay last night in the hotel at Te Kiri. Naturally I was told many times of your arrival."

"Oh . . ." Sharon found herself blushing. She could just imagine the knowing looks Brent had been getting in the Te Kiri hotel. How he would hate that.

Judith was explaining in a cool voice. "We invited Miss Denholm to stay the night as she had come all this way to see you and found you away."

Brent raised his eyebrows. "You expected me to be here?" he asked Sharon.

He was so cool she could not believe it was the same man with whom she had spent those wonderful few weeks. And immediately she was on the defensive.

"Yes. Yes, I did expect you to be here."

Judith went on explaining quietly. "Miss Denholm was near Te Kiri on holiday and she remembered that you had asked her to call if she was ever up this way so she came out on the launch . . ."

As though he controlled his irritation

with difficulty, Brent smiled, tardily. "I hope you are enjoying your visit. Judith has looked after you while I was not here to do it?"

"Oh, yes, of course. Everybody has been most kind."

"Nick tells me you are going back with him this afternoon."

She was taken aback at this. Nick had not seemed like a gossip and, yet, he, too, had apparently told Brent of her arrival.

"Nick told you I was here?"

"No. Shall we say I told him. I asked him if he was expecting a passenger at Warden's Cove."

Their eyes met. It was quite obvious that he could not wait to have her gone. Deep inside she was terribly hurt and humiliated, but she was too proud to let her emotions show.

She tilted her head independently. "I'm going back this afternoon."

Relief flooded his set face for a moment, until Judith intervened.

"But that's not necessary. Why don't you stay a few days? I saw you on the beach this morning. You were enjoying it.

Why don't you spend some of your holiday here? How long have you got?"

Sharon watched Brent's face and did not answer.

"How long have you got?" Judith asked again, and she replied in a low voice, "About two weeks."

"Then there's no need at all to rush away."

"I'm sure Miss Denholm has other plans," Brent argued, icily.

Sharon was torn two ways. Her pride demanded that she insist on leaving, an obstinate streak in her nature urged her to stay. This isn't Brent, she told herself. Something is terribly wrong and I can't go away and just leave him to sort it all out alone. He loves me, I know he does. There's something evil here that makes him like this.

"Wouldn't you like to stay with us for a while?" Judith asked. Her expression was kind, her voice solicitous, but Sharon was sure that she wanted to keep her there to observe her with Brent. He means so much to her, she thought, that she just has to know where I fit in the picture, even if she gets hurt knowing.

"Yes, I would like to stay if I may," she said.

Afterwards he made an excuse to be alone with her. She was on the porch, about to leave the house and wander down to the beach to meet Nick's launch to tell him that she would not be going back that day and to ask him to bring her suitcase, which she had left with her belongings at the Te Kiri hotel, the next day.

As she moved down the steps, she heard his voice.

"Sharon."

She turned round and he came out on to the porch.

"Yes, Brent?"

"I want to talk to you." He was deadly serious, there was just a touch of cold anger in his voice.

"I'm just going down to the jetty. Nick will be expecting me to go back this afternoon. And I want to ask him to bring some things out for me tomorrow as I'm staying on."

"You're determined to stay on?"

She turned away so that he should not see her face. "Yes. Why not? Judith seems

97

keen to have me stay." She moved down the steps and on to the drive away from him.

"I'll come part of the way with you. We won't get a chance to talk in the house."

She shrugged. "Just as you like."

They wandered down the drive and she was acutely conscious of being watched. She was sure that from the house someone's eyes observed their walk. Soon they were in the midst of the beautiful garden, hidden from the house by thick foliage. She relaxed a little and became more aware of him.

"What do you want to talk about?" She kept her voice calm.

"I would like to know what you are doing here." The words were clipped, and she was immediately on the defensive.

"And I would like to know why you didn't come to meet my parents; why you just disappeared."

She faced him bluntly, her eyes wide and questioning, and saw him wince slightly, his mouth grim. Quickly her anger evaporated. What is it Brent? she wanted to cry. Why are you like this? What are you trying to hide? Her whole body seemed to melt with overpowering affection for him, she yearned to touch him and, with the force of her love, frighten away this thing that lay between them.

"I had to do that, Sharon," he said. "I should have done it earlier."

"But why?"

"Don't ask me that. For your own sake just go away and forget about me." He was suddenly Brent as he had been. He was no longer angry or aloof.

"I can't do that, Brent. You know that. It's too late."

"It's not too late. You've only known me a few weeks. Nothing permanent can be built in a few weeks." Though the words implied that for him nothing permanent had sprung from their short association, she was not hurt. She was convinced that only his concern for her had made him say it.

"Is it something to do with Judith?"

"I can't tell you what it is," he answered, harshly.

"You were in love with her once, weren't you, Brent?"

"That's been over a long time."

Her heart leaped. She had almost been afraid that he was still in love with her. Poor Judith, who obviously loved him as much as she herself loved him. But why was it over? They had been in love apparently at the time of Margaret Warden's death. Could it possibly be that he had fallen out of love with Judith because she could not walk? It was an appalling thought and she pushed it from her.

"I must go. The *Louise* will be waiting for me."

"Sharon, I beg you not to stay."

She searched his face earnestly, yearning for understanding.

"I'm sorry, Brent, but I *am* staying. For a few days anyway."

She moved down the drive, out through the gate, across the fields, towards the jetty.

"You don't think I should stay, do you?" she said to Nick on the wharf.

"It's none of my business," he answered, deliberately being busy with the boat.

"I'm afraid I've annoyed you." She was genuinely contrite. "Is it because you keep calling in for me and I don't leave? I'm afraid I've put you to a lot of trouble."

"Forget it."

She was rebuffed and felt a little foolish. How ridiculous of her to imagine that what she did mattered to him. He was a man wrapped up in his own man's life; his launch, the sea; a man full of quiet confidence in himself; a man sufficient unto himself; certainly not a man who would take a casual interest in a girl he had known only a few days.

She did not feel happy as she went back to the house. She wanted to be alone to think and would have slipped upstairs to her room to puzzle over the things she had heard that day, but there was more to come. She was aware of a low mumble of voices as she mounted the stairs but, when she heard Judith's voice speak her name, she became rooted to the spot. She could not move though she knew she was eavesdropping.

"What is Sharon Denholm doing here?"

And, after a long silence, Brent's voice. "You invited her to stay."

"Oh, Brent, please don't bandy words with me. She came here to see you. She said you had asked her to come. Did you?"

Sharon could feel herself growing hot with embarrassment.

"I don't know," he said. "Perhaps I did." Sharon relaxed, weak with gratitude. "I met her on my trip. She works in a bank and was able to tell me something I wanted to know about the district. We talked quite a lot. I probably did invite her to call here some time."

Inwardly Sharon shrivelled up. He could dismiss it all so lightly.

"I didn't expect it to be this soon," the voice went on.

How coolly he lies, Sharon thought, then brutally thrust the thought away. It was her pride he was protecting with his lies and somehow she did not feel that he was doing it easily.

"Oh, Brent, is that really all there was to it?" Judith's voice was low and anguished.

"Of course. What else could there be?"

"I suspect that you are attracted to her."

There was a long silence. His voice was so low she could hardly hear it. "And if I am? Don't goad me too far, Judith."

Judith's voice shook as though she controlled it with great difficulty. "Brent, what has happened to us? Why are you doing this to me? We love each other, Brent. You can't deny that."

"Don't be a fool, Judith. Do you think there could ever be anything between us after what has happened?"

"But we couldn't help it. We couldn't help it . . ."

"Oh, there you are, Miss Denholm." Dorothy fluttered out of the kitchen and caught Sharon on the stairs. "Have you made arrangements with Nick to bring your things?" She stopped, becoming aware of Sharon's poised, listening attitude. She, too, froze; she stood as though she did not breathe. But the voices had stopped.

"What are you listening to?" Dorothy asked in a small, disembodied voice, her head cocked to one side in her characteristic gesture.

"Nothing, nothing at all," Sharon replied sharply, understanding her only too well, but feeling horribly guilty to be caught eavesdropping. "I'm just going up to my room."

Her mind was seething with impressions, words, people, and she urgently wanted to sort them all out, to try to understand something about this place, these people—and the night a year ago when Margaret Warden had plunged to her death. But she was interrupted again at the top of the first flight of stairs for, as she reached the landing, Danny appeared from the office where he apparently did his school lessons.

"I'm through with lessons for today," he told her brightly as he passed, then skidded to a halt on the stairs.

"I'm off for a swim in the creek. Wanna come?"

She responded with a quick smile. "I don't have a bathing suit."

"Auntie Judith'll lend you one."

"I . . . I don't really feel like swimming just now," she excused herself.

"Well, come for the ride."

"The ride?"

"Mm. I go on a horse. It's over some of the hills. Can you ride?"

She looked doubtful. "Just a bit. Is it a very quiet horse?"

"We c'n borrow Cole's. It's the quietest hack around here."

She had not particularly want to go. She was here for more important things than an impromptu visit to the creek, but he was being nice to her in a small-boy way, trying to entertain a guest and improve her holiday in the way he thought the most fun. This rather surprised her. Obviously she was a hit with Danny and she did not want to dampen his enthusiasm.

"All right," she said. "Why not? But will Cole lend me his horse?"

"Sure."

And so, wearing her own clothes again —the slacks and mended blouse of the day before—she found herself trudging across the paddocks with Danny and the dog towards the shepherd's cottage where Hank and Cole slept.

The doors of the cottage were wide open to the bright, summer afternoon, but there was no sign of life. Under a tree in the yard a dog howled, but that was all. At home, Danny marched inside calling for Hank and Cole without getting a reply. Sharon followed him rather hesitantly. The cottage was small, with a porch back and front, two bedrooms off a hall, a kitchenette and a sparsely furnished lounge in the front. Danny knew his way around and they finished up in the lounge. The room was a pleasant enough place with glass doors opening on to the front porch, but the décor was odd. A coiled rope hung on a nail on the wall which was smothered in picture cuttings relative to the American west. Several cowboy film stars and their horses were apparent and over the mantelpiece was a huge coloured picture of a cattle round-up. Several different types of rifles also adorned the walls.

In one corner of the room was a large, modern radiogram. Danny went across and looked at the record on the turntable.

"Do you like playing records?" he asked.

"Uhuh. What is it?"

"Buddy Elgar singing 'The Lone Prairie Star'."

Sharon began looking through a pile of records on the floor. "What else is there?"

"No use lookin' for anything different. They're all the same sort. Cole don't buy any other kinds."

Sharon sat back on her heels. "He really

does go for the wild west and all that, doesn't he?"

"Uhuh. This horse of this that he's going to lend you is called Silver."

She grimaced. "A grown man."

"Pardon?"

"Nothing. And what about Hank? Does he really go for all this, too?"

"He just does what Cole wants him to do," the boy replied with surprising insight.

"Why?"

"Aunt Dorothy says he's grateful to Cole for giving him a job. He'd been in jail, you know. What do you think about that?"

"I heard about that. It was for killing his wife I believe."

"Yes. Aunt Dorothy says she doesn't trust him. She says he looks like a man who'd kill his wife. She's afraid of him I reckon. But Dad says he's not likely to kill anybody else unless it was somebody all set to hurt Cole."

"You talking about us?"

Unheard Cole and Hank had entered the room behind them. Sharon started guiltily when she heard Cole's voice. How much had they heard? She stood up.

"I'm sorry. We shouldn't be in your house like this."

Cole watched her through narrowed lids; his face relaxed slightly as though he liked what he saw.

"That's all right. Danny comes in all the time."

Over Cole's shoulder she found herself looking into the quiet, brown eyes of Hank. They were set in such a young-old face that she was disconcerted. Here was a man who had ruthlessly killed a woman who had cheated him. She shuddered. The others seemed to accept him quite naturally; he was quiet and unobtrusive and, yet, somehow his shadow lay over the whole family. With his dark hair, olive skin and dark clothes the shadow became sinister.

"We came to borrow a horse," Sharon went on.

"Sure. Where y' goin'?"

"To the creek for a swim, Cole," Danny answered for her. He appeared completely unconcerned. The possibility of them having heard the previous conversation did not seem to worry him at all.

Cole reached forward and took the record she was holding from her hand.

"You like Buddy Elgar?" he asked, looking at the disc.

"Of course."

"That guitar of his is really something."

"Yes."

He picked up a guitar which stood up against the wall beside the radiogram. "Hank is hot stuff on the guitar," he said. "Show her, Hank."

Obediently Hank reached for the guitar but while his thin fingers searched the strings for the right chord he and Sharon shared a look, a brief understanding. He's really much more intelligent than Cole is, she told herself as he strummed the instrument, the guitar resting on one knee and his foot on a chair. He played very well and Sharon watched him ironically. It seemed a strange thing for a wife-killer to be doing.

"There. Doesn't he send you?" Cole demanded what he had finished.

Sharon smiled quietly but Danny agreed heartily. "That's neat."

The two men went outside with them to where Butch was asleep in the sun. Danny went off to fetch his own horse which was apparently grazing in a paddock behind the house. Cole brought his own horse forward for Sharon.

"Are you sure you don't mind?" she asked.

"She's all yours," he said. He looked at her with unconcealed admiration as she swung into the saddle and sat there easily, waiting for Danny to come back. "You sure look pretty on a horse. Ain't never seen a woman could sit on a horse properly before."

His accent was so pronounced she stifled a desire to laugh out loud. There was something about him that suggested he would not take kindly to being laughed at.

"You're just flattering me," she answered, using his own nasal intonation.

"Nope, I mean it."

Danny cantered up. He sat on his horse like one born to the saddle. As they moved off he turned back to Cole.

"Cole, will you bring up some films to show us tonight? Aunt Dorothy said to ask you. To entertain Sharon."

"Uhuh. Hope I've got something that will entertain the lady. You like westerns?" he asked Sharon.

"Oh, yes. I just love westerns." He was unaware of her sarcasm.

"It's a date then."

They moved off guiding the horses out through the gate, across the paddocks towards the foothills. Once Sharon twisted around in her saddle and looked back. The two figures of Cole and Hank still stood in the yard watching them go. She rode on thoughtfully, wondering about them.

8

AFTER they had all dined in the big panelled dining-room that evening, they moved into the lounge where Cole began, in leisurely fashion, to set up his equipment.

"It's very kind of you to bother like this for me," Sharon said to Aunt Dorothy. "But you mustn't worry about entertaining me . . ."

"Oh, but, of course, we must. There's not much to do in the evenings here. We don't have television and no picture theatre. We read a lot and play cards sometimes, and show home movies. Cole has quite a selection that he's taken himself over the years, and he usually has two or three out on hire."

They sat around in a semi-circle while they waited for Cole to begin. Judith sat quietly in her chair. Sharon could feel herself being watched by the quiet, shadowed eyes. She wondered what Judith was thinking and what she thought of

Cole's affability tonight. For Cole was being flatteringly genial towards Sharon. When he came into dinner he greeted her with a bright "Howdy" and asked after the ride to the creek. He jostled for a position by her at the table and kept her wants supplied.

With Cole out of hearing for a moment, Judith commented on this.

"You seem to have made quite a hit with Cole."

"Have I?"

"Yes. He's usually very terse. He's almost forgetting to be the hard-eyed gunslinger." She smiled briefly as she said it but her face was thoughtful.

"He's rather amusing, isn't he?" Sharon replied and watched the speculative look in Judith's eyes disappear. Judith was so transparent in her love for Brent that Sharon could follow her train of thought. She wants me to be interested in Cole, she thought. Judith's anxiety depressed her. I can't help it, she told herself. I love Brent, too. I don't want to hurt you, but I need him. I want him to love me.

"How about switching off those lights," Cole said to Hank who stood by the switch. In the brief moment before they were plunged into darkness Sharon became aware of Brent's worried and irritated frown upon her. He doesn't want to be bothered with this, she thought. And he just hates me being here. But, Brent, why?

The movies that followed were interspersed with polite, casual conversation. They were mostly films that Cole had hired from a camera shop, but one or two had been taken on the farm and included some of those present. Sharon preferred these to the commercial films. During one that had been taken on the beach apparently while a picnic was in progress she relaxed in the darkness enjoying observing Brent, lithe and brown in bathing togs waving a nonchalant hand at the camera. One by one the people in the room were caught in holiday mood, staring self-consciously into the lens, waving the camera away. And there was Judith, splashing into the sea, looking not much different from now, slim and eye-catching in a royal blue bathing suit. Judith moving around gracefully. The momentum of this suddenly struck Sharon with terrific force.

The film had been taken before the accident and death of Margaret. Of course. Danny had said there had been no picnics on the beach since his mother died. As the others in the room were struck by the implications of the film there was a pulsating silence. Looking at Judith Sharon saw her sitting upright in her chair, grasping the arms with white knuckles. For the first time Sharon was blindingly aware of what it must mean to Judith, who had been the girl in the picture, to be tied to the inactivity of the chair.

The tension grew with each second and Sharon found herself staring at the screen. Something was going to happen. The others were waiting for it as though paralyzed.

The roving eye of the camera moved across the beach suddenly jerking itself backwards in an inexperienced hand to focus on a woman wearing a sun dress and clasping a beach ball. She was standing with her bare feet in water at the waves' edge, laughing. Though she was a woman of about thirty her hair was girlishly caught up in a pony tail. She was a woman attractive enough but surprisingly ordinary when one remembered that she was Judith's sister. For Sharon was telling herself this even while her mind groped for the woman's identity. Margaret! She stared hard at the picture watching the carefree energy of the woman as she played on the beach, searching her face—for what? A clue to the answer to the riddle of her death? Slowly the camera went nearer and suddenly the face was filling the screen. It was an empty face and Sharon could not feel that she knew the woman at all.

"For God's sake, turn it off!"

Brent's voice shattered the strained silence. He groped his way to the light switch and turned it on. As the bright light flooded the room the image faded. Slowly, Cole switched off the machine.

Blinking a little in the sudden light, Sharon looked around the group. Brent stood in the corner his hand still on the switch, his back to the company as though he strove to gain control of himself. Aunt Dorothy, a distant look on her face, sat with her hands folded in her lap staring at the blank screen. Judith leaned back in her

116

chair with her eyes closed, exhausted. At the back of the room hovered the dark shadow of Hank. Sharon felt a quick surge of sympathy for Danny when she saw him sitting bolt upright in his chair with tears in his eyes. As he saw her look he became ashamed of them and brushed his eyes with the back of his hand, pointedly staring away in another direction. How cruel, she thought. How cruel. She looked at Cole. He stood behind the projector, his eyes narrowed, his expression inscrutable.

Brent turned around, his hands clenched into fists, his face tight. "Damn you, Cole. You did that on purpose." His face was tortured.

"Did I?" Cole drawled.

But he had done it on purpose, Sharon was certain, and the sudden sight of Margaret on the screen had disconcerted them all. Why did Brent mind so much? He had not loved his wife if the stories she had heard were true. He had loved Judith. Why did Cole do it? What an enigma he was. He had enjoyed hurting Brent.

Yes, Cole was an enigma.

Later that night when the household

had all retired to their beds she went out to the balcony, hugging a quilted dressing-gown around her in the cooler night air. She wanted to think, to sort out her impressions of the household, to try to understand something about Brent and his wife's death.

She looked down into the garden and breathed in the night air. In the shadows she could see Butch lying outside his kennel, shuffling restlessly in his sleep.

She did not see the shadow of a man thrown on the wall behind her, the hands reaching out. She was unaware of any presence other than her own until she was caught roughly in two strong arms. She twisted violently and opened her lips to scream, but before she could utter a sound a large hand clamped over her mouth.

"Don't scream. I won't hurt you," said Cole's voice in her ear.

She struggled again to free herself from his embrace, but one arm pinioned her against his chest, his other hand was still clamped across her mouth.

"Go on, struggle," he whispered and she wondered if he was laughing at her. "I like it."

She ceased to struggle and stood absolutely still, waiting to find out what he intended to do. Her worst fears were realized for, after a moment or two, he released her mouth and his own came down hard on her bruised lips. She twisted her head to avoid him, his mouth slipped away and found her neck. She was free to scream, but she did not. The situation was impossible. If she screamed and the whole family came running, her shaky welcome in the house would surely be undermined. Cole would, of course, deny that he had touched her. Whether they believed her or not she would have to leave in the morning. And she did not want to leave while nothing was settled with Brent.

Down in the garden, Butch growled. She twisted and turned while Cole's lips moved across the hollow of her throat into the folds of her dressing-gown. But misunderstanding her quiescence, he was careless and loosened the grip he had on her. She pulled herself violently free and with all the force she could muster slapped him hard across the face with her bare hand. He slumped back against the balcony railings, nursing his jaw in baffled surprise.

And at that moment a door along the balcony opened and a figure glided through. Sharon's breath went out of her body in an audible gasp until she realized that it was Aunt Dorothy in her trance-like state. She stood on the balcony, apparently oblivious to them, listening.

"Don't you ever do that again," Sharon told Cole tightly. She glanced nervously towards Aunt Dorothy.

"Don't take any notice of her," he said, straightening up, his ardour cooled by the force of her attack. "She's bats."

She turned back to him, furiously, feeling the heat of his lips against her skin. "If you ever do that again, I'll . . . I'll . . ."

"You'll what? You'll complain to Brent, I suppose."

"Yes. Yes, I will."

"And d'ya think he'd care? He's not in love with you. He's crazy about Judith. He fell for her when she was a kid in pigtails around the place."

She felt as though she drowned in a dash of icy cold water when he said it. Her heart cried out in disbelief.

"That's not true," she protested.

"It's true all right. And can y' blame him. She's quite a dish is Judith."

"If they are in love they'd get married." She hated herself for standing there arguing with him, but she yearned to be reassured, to have him deny his own words.

"They're just biding their time. Brent's being very, very careful. The police asked some pretty nosy questions when Margaret was pushed off this balcony."

"Pushed?"

"Y'don't really think she fell, do you?"

"She was an epileptic. She could easily have taken a bad turn and fallen against the railing."

His eyes narrowed and he nodded slowly, sardonically, as though he found the comment ludicrous. "She was an epileptic all right, and you know what they're like to live with? Sheer hell, gorgeous. Sheer hell."

Sharon thought of the laughing woman in the picture that night. She had seemed pleasant enough.

"Oh, sure," he went on as if he could read her thoughts. "She was okay that day on the beach. She was often okay, but she was moody. She'd go for days sometimes not speaking to anybody. Other times she'd fly into a rage for nothin' at all. I tell you she gave Brent a time. Yeah, she sure gave Brent hell."

This was such a change from the picture of Margaret that Sharon had formed in her own mind, that she was startled into silence.

"Everybody in Te Kiri knew Brent was making heavy hay with Judith. The cops were suspicious, but they couldn't do much. Judith had her story ready and she stuck to it. But Brent is too shrewd to turn round and marry her the next minute."

"But Judith fell off the balcony too."

"Yeah."

"That disproves everything you're saying."

"You think so?" His mouth curled.

"Even in your warped mind, you couldn't think that Brent would push Judith off. That wouldn't make sense."

"I think Judith saw it happen and tried to prevent Margaret falling. Then she kept quiet to shield my skunk of a brother." Strangely, in the half-light his face softened a little. "Judith is different from Brent. She wouldn't hurt a fly."

Aunt Dorothy glided towards them quite unaware of their conversation. "Can you hear it?" she whispered.

"There's nothing to hear, Aunt Dorothy," Sharon answered. "Let me take you back to bed." To Cole she said, "I don't believe you, Cole. I don't believe anything you've suggested to me. Even if Brent . . . Brent meant nothing to me, I couldn't believe it. It's not a strong enough motive for . . . for murder. Divorce is too easy."

"You think so? Margaret would never have given Brent a divorce and he couldn't divorce her without grounds. Believe me she had Brent tied. He couldn't even walk out on her. He wouldn't leave Warden's Cove for anything, not even Judith."

Sharon led Aunt Dorothy back into the house, but there was an awful doubt in her mind. Cole had been sincere. He had even forgotten to use his accent.

9

"THE *Louise* has got engine trouble."

They were all out on the patio enjoying morning coffee the next morning when Danny came sprinting round the side of the house. It was warm and humid with white, cotton-wool clouds decorating the blue sky.

Sharon sat up straight. Somehow she felt proprietary about the *Louise*.

"The *Louise*?" they echoed.

"Yep. Nick's got to work on her before she'll go any further. I told him to come up for some coffee and he says he will in a minute."

Aunt Dorothy smiled wryly. "Oh, you did, did you?"

"Yep. So can you make some more, Aunt Dorothy? He won't be able to stay long. He's got to get the *Louise* fixed."

He was gone again, back to meet Nick. Aunt Dorothy went into the house to make more coffee and Sharon went in to help her. When she came back out carrying the coffee-pot and another cup and saucer on a tray, she found Danny was back and Nick with him. He stood up as he saw her and advanced to take the tray from her. She smiled warmly at him quite unaware that for a moment they created a little circle of intimacy that was not missed by those present.

"What's wrong with the *Louise*?" she asked him, her face concerned for his boat.

"I don't know yet. I'm still tinkering with it."

She poured him out a cup of coffee and he relaxed easily in a cane chair. With her entrance, there was suddenly a subtle difference in the atmosphere; she could feel it herself but could not define it. It had something to do with the way Nick's eyes followed her round, the way he seemed to listen more intently when she contributed to the light conversation. It became disconcerting after a while. She felt she was the cynosure of all their eyes.

He seemed reluctant to go but admitted that he could only spare a few minutes as he was already behind on the run and still had to locate the trouble and put it right.

As he stood up to go, Judith suggested lightly, "Why don't you go on the run with Nick, Sharon? He'll be back by dinner-time tonight. It would be quite interesting and entertaining for you."

For a moment Sharon studied her briefly and her aim was transparent. I know what you are trying to do, she thought. You want to throw us together. You want me to get interested in someone other than Brent. She could not see that Judith had already sensed that Nick was attracted to her.

"Yes, why don't you come?" Nick agreed.

"Thank you. I'd love to."

"Can I go too?" Danny begged. "Please, Nick. I haven't been for ages."

Before Nick could reply, Judith answered him. "Not today, Danny. Nick will take you another time perhaps. There's a new batch of school work in the mail bag and that must come first."

"Aw, Aunt Judith." Danny appealed to another source. "Aunt Dorothy, can't I go?"

"No, dear. Not if Judith thinks you'd best not. Now, be a good boy and don't

126

argue with us. There'll be lots of other trips."

"I hope to cast off within an hour," Nick told Sharon.

But it was half past one and he had been back to the house for lunch before he was able to start the engine of the *Louise*. Sharon stood on the jetty and waited for him, wearing the slim-fitting slacks and a shirt blouse.

"Will you be warm enough?" he asked her. "There's some cloud coming up and if the sun gets blacked out it'll probably turn cold."

"I've got a jumper with me. It's in here with the sandwiches Miss Warden made me bring." She held up a large tote bag.

As the boat chugged away from the jetty out to the open sea it did indeed suddenly get cooler and she was glad, as she shared the cockpit with him, to pull on the green jumper.

"Don't you feel cold?" she asked him as he stood at the wheel in his shirt sleeves.

"I'm used to it. I don't feel the cold much—or the heat." He turned his head towards her as if what he would say next was of importance. "It's my dark blood I guess."

Her expression did not change. "Lucky you," she said.

After a moment he went on, "You look almost dark enough to own some Maori blood yourself."

She lifted her hair out from the polo-necked collar of the jumper with both hands.

"I'm afraid not. Wish I could say I had, but my parents both came out from England in their teens."

The clouds scudded across the sun and a chill breeze played with the sea, but she began to enjoy herself. Overhead a seagull hovered, then swooped downwards for an unsuspecting fish. He knew all about the coastline and its history and he punctuated the conversation with some interesting anecdotes. Sometimes there were no jetties in the bays and men came out to them in motor-propelled boats for the supplies Nick had on board. It was a long trip along the coast. What a wonderful life he led, she thought, and wondered how he made it pay.

As if he had read her mind, he said, "I

suppose you wonder how I make a living at this."

"How did you guess? But what a wonderful time you have."

"I'm not rich, but it pays fairly well. I'm heavily subsidized by the Government as a mail run. The parcels and passengers all help. Sometimes I get quite a number of tourists all at once who just come along for the ride. I even do a bit of fishing commercially. It all adds up. And I use the boat on Sundays in the summer months for anyone who wants to hire her for deep-sea fishing, any specific trips, or for just a day out. I do all right."

"It sounds very pleasant."

Towards the end of the run the weather became worse. The clouds had banked up to a dark, lowering mass, the breeze had strengthened to a strong wind, the frisky little waves became choppy and sullen.

Nick looked at the dark sky. "There's a storm brewing."

As he spoke the words the first drops of rain fell; large drops that splashed on to the cabin roof, the deck, and into the cockpit. The sky was suddenly streaked with lightning. They waited and there was a loud clap of thunder. The rain increased. Sitting in the cockpit, Sharon clutched the side of the boat for support as it rolled with a wave.

"Go into the cabin out of the wet," Nick ordered her. "We'll put into a bay while this blows over."

With difficulty she made her way into the cabin. The rain drummed on the roof. It was cosy and warm inside. She sat down on the bunk and waited. The boat pitched and rolled in the heavy sea. She felt a twinge of nausea in the depths of her stomach. After a while she staggered to the cabin door and looked outside. Wearing a waterproof coat and hat in the driving rain, Nick was tying the *Louise* up to a jetty. When he saw her he climbed back into the cockpit.

"Where are we?" she asked him as another flash of lightning lit the sky.

"It's a place called Benson's Bay."

"I'm ashamed to admit that I feel queer," she told him ruefully.

"We'll go ashore until it blows over. Here put this on." He tossed her another waterproof coat from behind the door. She struggled into it. It was much too large for her. "You wear this," he said and gave her his hat. She tried to protest but he insisted and so she pulled it over her hair.

"Bring your bag with the Thermos and sandwiches," he ordered her as he thrust some things into a canvas bag. With the rain driving in their faces they made their way along the jetty and on to the beach. Sharon looked about for the usual homestead, but the only building in sight was a small shack under some huge macro carpa trees.

"Where do the Bensons live?" she asked.

"Nobody lives here now," he answered, shouting above the noise of thunder and wind. "The Bensons built a new house in the next bay and the old place was pulled down. Come on." He caught her hand and pulled her after him across the beach, through a wet paddock towards the hut. "There's only this empty rabbiter's hut but it'll be dry," he shouted.

The door opened easily. The windows were misty with dirt, cobwebs, and rain, and inside it was only half-light. As her eyes grew accustomed to the darkness Sharon could see the bare, unlined walls, a shaky wooden table, a chip-heater in one corner with a blackened chimney rising through the roof, and a stained and chipped sink along one wall.

They pulled off the wet raincoats and hung them on some nails behind the door. From his canvas bag Nick pulled out a rug and laid it out on the wooden floor.

"Shall we sit down and have a cup of coffee and a bite to eat?" he asked with mock formality.

She laughed and settled down on the rug and opened the bag with the food and drink that Aunt Dorothy had thoughtfully provided. Everything was there—even an extra cup. In picnic style they relaxed on the rug while Sharon poured the coffee. Outside the heavy rain beat a tattoo on the iron roof, threw handfuls of spray at the dirty windows. He sat with his knees drawn up holding the cup of coffee in his long, brown fingers. She felt curiously free and at home with him. He was a man to inspire confidence. How could she, then, have come to believe what she did?

They talked lightly about his life at sea and her life at home and the daily grind at the bank.

"I met Brent when he came into the bank," she admitted without thinking after a while.

Something new was immediately added to the atmosphere, a tension, an awareness.

"Yes?" He waited as if she must add more. Her hand tightened on the cup she held and she looked away. She was quite suddenly overcome with the desire to share it all with another person; to tell someone else everything; someone who was an outsider who could look at it all dispassionately. She wanted to hear someone laugh at her when she told them that she suspected Brent had killed his wife. It was the first time she had admitted it even to herself and the conscious thought jolted her. No, I don't think that, she argued silently with herself. I don't. But a small inner voice of caution argued back and she knew that she would be glad to hear Nick tell her how ridiculous that was.

She felt there were no barriers between them at that moment. "Can I tell you about it?" she asked him quietly.

He understood her mood, that what he

would hear was a personal thing. "If you want to."

"Yes. Yes, I do want to." And so she told him about her meeting with Brent and of the weeks that followed. She omitted nothing. "I fell in love with him you see," she told him, watching his face as she did so. His expression did not alter. "And I thought he loved me." Without rancour she told him about the night he had evaded meeting her family. "I was afraid Kerry would take him from me," she said. "She is awfully stiff competition—Kerry. But it was Brent I should have been afraid of, not Kerry." Calmly she told him how she had come to look for Brent, without shame. And then she stopped.

"And what did Brent have to say for himself?" he asked watching her levelly.

"He . . . he hedged. He wants me to forget about him. For my own sake, he says. It sounds like a brush-off, doesn't it?"

"I suppose it does."

"But there's much more to it than that. Something is wrong at Warden's Cove. They're all so mixed up. Judith worships Brent. You can see it in her face. And Cole

134

hates him. I feel he would harm him if he could. And Hank, the shepherd, would do anything for Cole. He would commit a murder for Cole, Brent has apparently said."

"Why would anyone say that? That seems an odd thing to say."

"Yes, but murder seems to be a word that fits Warden's Cove. I get the strangest feeling that they are all secretly harbouring the word but that they won't say it out loud. I don't think Margaret Warden fell off the balcony at all. I think she was pushed off. Someone killed her."

He watched her quizzically. "Don't you think that that would have occurred to the police? If there had been any slight suspicion of it . . ."

"But Judith insisted that she fell . . ."

"Yes. You think she's lying about it?"

"Yes. Yes, I do."

"But why would she do that?"

"To protect someone. Brent perhaps."

"You think Brent pushed his wife off the balcony?"

Her eyes widened. She was horrified at herself and the words that had come almost unbidden. "Oh, no! What am I saying? I don't think so at all. He wouldn't do that. I know he wouldn't. It's not in his nature to resort to violence."

"And how do you know it isn't? You don't really know him very well." He was watching her carefully, giving her all his attention. She moved restlessly and bit her lip.

"No, I don't know him very well. And yet I feel as if I've known him all my life. He's good and . . . gentle. He wouldn't do it."

"Then why have you even had such a doubt? Something must have put the idea into your head. The police have accepted the accident as . . . an accident."

"But there are things the police weren't told."

"Such as?"

"Danny tells me he saw a third person on the balcony when Margaret fell. He was out in the garden trying to quieten that dog of his. It barked you see and woke everybody up. But afterwards no one else mentioned the person whoever it was and the police were not told of it. Danny told Brent about it and he told the boy not to mention it either. Don't you think that's suspicious?"

"It might be, but people often have innocent-enough reasons for doing the strangest things."

"Yes, but as Cole pointed out, why, if he loved Judith, hasn't he married her now that they are both free?"

He did not answer her question, but asked one of his own. "You've been discussing it with Cole?"

She felt herself colour as she remembered Cole on the balcony. Her eyes became remote and thoughtful as she murmured assent. He was watching her intently and, suddenly, his voice became sharper. "What are you thinking about?"

She winced, startled, and came back from a long distance. "I . . . what do you mean?"

"You had a strange expression in your eyes. Talking about Cole reminded you of something, didn't it? What was it?"

"I don't know what you mean."

He was silent for a while as though he regretted this show of interest in her affairs, this forcing of her confidence. "Be careful of Cole," he warned at last. "Cole is a dangerous man. There's a nasty temper lurking beneath that cowboy's exterior."

"You know him well?"

"Everybody in Te Kiri knows him well. Used to go into town often at one time. Gets a few drinks in and is spoiling for a fight. Many's the time Dan Andrews, the local cop, has been called into the bar to break up a scrap with Cole in it. It got so bad that Brent had to clamp down on him and keep him out of town. That's another reason he hates Brent. He doesn't like being pushed around, but, whether he likes it or not, Brent's got the upper hand because he owns Warden's Cove. Either Cole co-operates or gets out. Sober he's not so bad, but drunk he's a menace. And he fancies himself as a ladies' man . . ."

Despite herself she felt the colour rise in her face again. Really, this was so silly. Why should she care if this Nick Kane knew that Cole had attempted to make love to her?

"You look as if he's already made a pass at you."

But now she had her emotions under

control and she smiled briefly. "Something like that."

But he did not smile. "How long are you going to stay there?" he asked.

She shrugged. "I don't know. I'm supposed to start work in not much more than a week. Judith just invited me to stay more or less for the whole holiday."

"Is there any point in that?" He waited a moment. "You came to see Brent and you've seen him."

"I came to find out why he walked out on me. But he avoids telling me why. He doesn't want to discuss it. He just wants me to leave. But I won't go until I know what's behind it all."

"And if you suspect there's a murder behind it all, do you really think it's safe to stay on?"

"Perhaps it's just all my imagination. But they all act so strangely. Aunt Dorothy keeps wandering around in the night, hearing heaven-knows-what. 'Can't you hear it?' she keeps asking. But she doesn't even know herself what it is. Something that happened that night is stuck somewhere in the recesses of her mind. And why would Cole want to make me think his own brother had murdered his wife? Surely he can't hate him that much." In her mind she was back at Warden's Cove and she told him all she could remember about the last few days not omitting Cole's advances on the balcony. He listened; his face remote. "That was when he made a pass at me," she told him smiling slightly.

"I think it would be a good idea to get away from the place," he told her rather grimly. "Cole's not a man to trifle with."

"But I can't go yet. I must stay until I know where I stand with Brent. That's not very ladylike, is it?" she asked, ruefully, then became suddenly serious again. "I'm not in the habit of . . . of chasing, shall we say? . . . men in this uninhibited way, but this is terribly important to me. I'm in love with him and I know he loves me. I've just got to make him admit it. If I go now I'll never see him again."

His eyes narrowed and his mouth was grim. She felt suddenly afraid of what he was going to say. Then, as if he had controlled his words with great difficulty, he withdrew and was quiet.

A strong gust of wind shook the shack

and she looked about apprehensively. She began to pack up the cups and the remains of the sandwiches and noticed that they had talked so long that the afternoon had begun to wane.

"Shouldn't we be going?" she asked. "It must be getting late. Do you think anyone will be worrying about us?"

"I doubt it. The Wardens know that I often put in at a bay in a storm. They won't expect us back with this raging." He stood up and went across to the window, peered through the dirty glass. "It looks to me as if it's set in for the night."

"What does that mean?"

"We might have to wait until it passes over which might not be till tomorrow."

She looked around the little room and back towards him. It was much darker in the shack than it had been earlier and she suddenly felt a little worried. To spend the night here with this man who was almost a stranger? What did she know about him after all? A few days ago she had not known he existed. And she was struck by the thought that he was a man of the sea and as such must have studied the weather reports. It was most unlikely that the storm had really caught him unprepared. He must have known it was due and knowing had still brought her with him.

"You stay here," he told her. "I'll go back to the *Louise* and bring some blankets to make us more comfortable through the night."

"Blankets?" Their eyes met. "You mean it really is necessary to stay here."

"I think so." He studied her for a moment. "You're not afraid to spend the night here with me, are you?"

"Of course not."

He pulled on his waterproof and she watched from the window as he made his way across the wet grass towards the jetty, carrying the canvas bag. She felt a ridiculous desire to run from the shack, outside into the rain; anywhere. She felt trapped. She was convinced that he had engineered the whole thing. But the *Louise* was the only way out of the bay and she could not get out alone. Watching through the window, she saw him coming back along the jetty and her vulnerable mouth tightened. I won't let him touch me, she told herself.

He pushed open the door and came in

dripping wet so that he was soon standing in a small pool of water. He removed his wet coat and the waterproof hat and hung them behind the door on a rusty nail. Then he was almost on his knees in front of the old stove, lighting a reluctant fire with some provisions he had brought from the boat.

"It will get cold a bit later," he said.

He was well equipped. Almost as if he had planned it, she told herself, ironically. The canvas bag had yielded cushions and blankets, and he had brought provisions to provide a hot drink, and something in a tin that he heated in a small saucepan on the stove. She was withdrawn and bitter, and ready for battle. The day turned into night and the only light in the shack was from the orange teeth of the stove. She knew it must be about ten o'clock and she was desperately tired after the sea air and the fitful nights of late. He tried to make conversation but she answered only in monosyllables. Silently, she called herself a fool over and over. To have been tricked into this! He began to arrange two beds on the floor with the blankets and cushions.

"It's time we turned in," he said. "I can see you're tired."

She clenched her fists with tension, waiting for something to happen, but he settled himself on one of the make-shift beds casually enough.

"Don't be nervous if you hear anything on the roof in the night. There's probably a 'possum or two about. I've got a torch handy."

She murmured something indistinguishable and tried to relax in the other bed. Though nothing had happened, she still could not trust him. I won't sleep, she insisted to herself. I'll stay awake all night. She lay on her back staring unblinkingly at the ceiling, determined not to doze off. After a while his breathing became heavier and she decided he had fallen asleep. Or was he feigning? She did not know what to expect and her heart was throbbing uncomfortably.

The next thing she knew was when she woke briefly. The room was still in darkness. Half asleep she struggled to remember where she was and became aware of him hovering over her. She shivered and realized that she was icy-cold.

144

"You'll all uncovered. You must be freezing," he said calmly and adjusted the rug, tucking it round her. "I've been outside after a 'possum," he went on. "Didn't you hear it on the roof?"

"No."

"It's stopped raining. We'll be able to get away as soon as it's dawn."

He moved away and she dozed again. The next time she awoke it was daylight. Weak sunlight struggled into the room through the murky windows. She sat up slowly and looked about. He was already up and stood only a few feet away, stuffing their gear into the canvas bag. Her body felt limp from the tension of the night before and she merely sat observing him for a moment.

He grinned. "Hi. You're awake."

"Yes."

"They weren't very comfortable beds, were they? How'd you sleep?"

"I slept all right."

"It's a wonderful day. The sun is shining and the sea's like a mill pond. I'll go on to the *Louise* and start breakfast going. I'll come back for that gear."

He would have gone but, now, she was

ashamed for what she had thought of him, and, yet, she was sure he would have known about the storm.

"Nick . . ."

He turned round and came back. "Yes?"

"You knew that storm was due, didn't you?"

He nodded slowly.

"You knew we would have to put ashore and stay the night even before we left Warden's Cove, didn't you?"

"Sure."

"But . . . but why?"

"I wanted the opportunity to be alone with you, that's why."

"But for what? You haven't . . . I mean you, well, you haven't attempted anything . . . ?"

He grinned, ruefully. "It was just an opportunity to get to know you better. When Judith started suggesting that you come with me, I couldn't resist it. Did you think my intentions were dishonourable?"

She looked up quickly to see if he was mocking her.

"I suppose I did."

"I wouldn't take advantage of a girl in

a situation like this. No, I just wanted to talk to you . . ." He stopped, thoughtfully. "Of course, I couldn't know that you were going to tell me how you stand with Brent Warden." His face closed up. "That puts a rather different light on things . . ."

"How do you mean?" she asked, earnestly, but something in his expression stopped her carrying the conversation further. For a moment words hovered in the air between them and she felt she was on the brink of some discovery but could not imagine what it was. She was afraid of how he might answer her.

She rose and began to roll up her bedding. They tidied the room in silence. Their relationship seemed to have moved into a different sphere.

10

NICK had said that no one would worry about them, that the people at Warden's Cove would know he had put into a bay for the night. But Sharon still felt a little worried about the return to the cove. Would they know that it was an uninhabited bay in which they had spent the night? Might they not suspect Nick's actions as she herself had done? She was sure that she could not bear it if Brent thought they had spent the night alone in a hut in an uninhabited bay, even though this had happened. This thought rather shocked her for surely there could be no love without trust.

Dorothy and Danny and his dog were all at the wharf to meet them and there was a lot of talking as they made their way up to the house. Judith, it seemed, had sent a message that Nick was to stay for lunch. She wants to see what progress has been made, Sharon told herself, with irony.

Danny went on ahead and they could hear him calling out that the *Louise* had arrived, as they neared the house. Sharon began to feel decidedly nervous at the thought of facing Brent. At the same time she desperately wanted to explain to him, to assure him that, though they had been alone all night, nothing had happened. More than anything else she feared that he would not care one way or another, but this was a thought she thrust from her. He must care because he loved her, she told herself.

She could not analyze her emotions when Brent immediately came out to meet them and found a way of being alone with her. She was startled to see that he looked tired, somehow defeated. His eyes looked weary and for the first time he appeared not to have shaved that morning. All her maternal instincts seemed to rise to the surface at his tortured appearance and she had never loved him so much.

"Brent, what's the matter?"

"The matter?" He looked at her as if he were thinking of something else.

"Yes. You look terrible."

"I didn't sleep so well last night," he

replied in a clipped voice. Then abruptly, "Where were you?"

She avoided his eyes. "It was a place called . . . Benson's Bay or some such name."

"The site of the old homestead?"

"Yes."

"I thought it must have been an isolated bay. Otherwise you would have phoned."

"We happened to be there when the storm got out of hand," she faltered.

His mouth twisted cynically. "You think so? Kane knows this coast like the back of his own hand. He could have brought the boat back here, storm or no storm."

"I felt ill . . ."

"Certainly he could have berthed where there was a homestead and people, if he had wanted to."

She looked away, unwilling to lie, but surprised to find that she wanted to defend Nick to him. Almost as if she felt possessive about Nick.

"He didn't want to, did he?" he went on.

She turned to face him again. "I can't understand you, Brent. Why this sudden interest in what I'm doing? You've been

150

cool enough since I got here. All you wanted to do was get rid of me." There was a bitter note in her voice.

"I want you to go home for your own sake."

"What do you mean? Please, please Brent tell me what you really mean."

He hesitated for a moment. "It might be dangerous for you to be here," he said, slowly.

"Dangerous?"

"Yes."

"But why?"

"I . . . I can't answer that. Just trust me and go home, Sharon."

"But I want to know why? It has something to do with your wife's death, hasn't it? Please, please Brent tell me what really happened that night."

"You know what happened."

"But I don't. I only know what everybody says happened." She was struggling to create an intimate atmosphere, to bring back the man he had been in the weeks when she had first known him, but now his face had closed against her and any slight advantage she might have had was lost.

"Let's go inside," he said, abruptly. "They will be wondering where we are."

She followed him meekly, but her mind seethed. What was it that Brent did not want her to know? It would be dangerous for her to stay, he had said. But who would want to hurt her? Why should she be afraid of any one of them? Unless perhaps Cole? The mysterious brooding Hank she could not fathom, and he had, of course, killed his wife, but that did not mean that he would harm her. He had absolutely no reason, no reason at all. Unless she hurt Cole in some way of course. But Cole was a person she intended to keep away from.

To add to the confusion in her mind she found that Judith in her quiet, determined way had planned a party for that evening and was insisting on Nick being there.

"Just a few people from the near-by bays," she explained. "It's Saturday night and you don't have the run to do tomorrow. You will be welcome to stay here the night."

"I've got to go back to town . . ."

"Yes, but you could come back this evening, couldn't you? And bring your guitar," she persisted. "Please do. One of the Hickmotts from the next bay has a saxophone. It would be fun to make music. We'll make a bed up for you."

"I can sleep on the *Louise*."

"Well, if you'd rather. But you will come, won't you?"

He studied Sharon, standing beside Brent, for a moment.

"Thank you. All right."

Sharon smiled a little cynically to herself. Judith was just too transparent. But she was troubled. Judith could see the attention Sharon got from the owner of the *Louise*. But can't she see that he's only looking for a mild flirtation, that men are like that? Sharon asked herself, quite used to only a luke-warm interest from men that quickly changed its loyalty when Kerry came into view.

How different the house suddenly became that evening. Until then it had appeared silent, mysterious, almost haunted. But, when about eight o'clock the guests started to arrive in boats of various kinds so that the quiet bay was dotted with small seacraft, the house took on new life. From every window lights blazed into the oncoming night. It would soon be dark and the garden lay bathed in shadow. All the doors and windows were open to catch the slight sea-breeze for, after the storm, it was hot again.

There were about twenty people at the party including Nick looking particularly attractive in a new garden-coloured shirt and summer slacks, and Hank slicked up and tidy in a dark, pin-striped suit that had seen better days. There was a farm-hand from five miles along the coast with an electric guitar and Desmond Hickmott from the next bay with a saxophone. As he had been inveigled into doing Nick had brought his guitar. Sharon was surprised to find that Judith was an expert on the piano. Although her feet could not pump the pedals she played delicately and with feeling. The saxophonist got quite excited after he had asked her to play a jazz piece and she had obliged with a very attractive rendering of "St. Louis Blues". The four musicians combined to make music and the others, drinks in hands, milled around the lounge, sometimes listening, some-times indulging in conversation. From an armchair across the room, Sharon watched Aunt Dorothy moving around the visitors, animatedly discussing gardens and plants with one or two, and all the time keeping a watchful, maternal eye on Judith and her needs. Obviously Judith was like her own child to the unmarried Dorothy. And it was easy to understand why. Judith was so gentle, so very sweet faced, so composed and uncomplaining in her disability. But was this the real self she showed the world? Was she like that underneath? Apparently Dorothy thought so. And she knows her so much better than me, Sharon argued with herself. And she knows that Judith took Brent from Margaret, but that does not seem to lower Judith in her estimation. And whatever Margaret was like, she was Judith's own sister.

Cole was leaning over the back of Nick's chair listening to the rhythm of his guitar with a far-away look in his eyes. Every time the band finished a number he demanded that they play one of his favourite western songs. Sharon watched him, amused, listening as he joined in in rather a shaky baritone as they played. She did not quite know what to make of Cole.

She looked around for Hank and remembered that Cole had sent him back to what he called the bunkhouse to get his guitar.

Suddenly Judith changed the beat and one or two younger couples stood up and began to twist. Across the room Cole looked up and caught Sharon watching him. Deliberately he moved across to her.

"Wanna dance?"

"Oh . . . No, thanks."

"You mean you can't twist?"

"Not very well." She smiled ironically. "I would have thought the square dance would have been more in your line."

"The square dance?" he asked uncomprehending. "What do you mean, the square dance?"

"Never mind." She could see Nick watching them and was suddenly disconcerted. Might he misunderstand her apparent friendliness to Cole? Men had many times misunderstood her sense of humour and interest in people.

It was a well-behaved party. Up to now no beer had been spilt on the carpet or in the top of the open piano. The small crowd was behaving itself. No one had stamped out a cigarette on the carpet or disappeared outside with someone else's wife. Cole smelt rather strongly of drink and she was rather dismayed to see that he was nonchalantly clasping a glass of what looked like gin. She remembered what Nick had said about Cole's character when he had had too much to drink and she hoped he would stay sober. She did not want to find herself coping with him in an amorous and fighting mood.

As if the thought had transferred itself to Cole, he stayed with her; sitting on the arm of her chair, pestering her with suggestions that they go and look at the moon together or wasn't she too durn hot in here and wouldn't she like to cool off outside?

Ironically she told him she thought it might be warmer out than in. Without humour, he did not see the point.

She was glad when it was time to go and help Aunt Dorothy in the kitchen with the supper. Though Aunt Dorothy protested politely and tried to insist that she go back and enjoy the party, she was glad to stay and avoid Cole.

Together they did the last preparations for supper, whipping cream and piling it on cakes that Dorothy had baked that afternoon, arranging the savouries on trays to reheat in the oven.

"I'm afraid this party has meant a lot of work for you," Sharon protested when she saw the food the other had prepared. There was a strange look in Dorothy Warden's eyes, the same nervous apprehension that she had shown when she had been forced to invite Sharon to stay at the cove. Sharon guessed that it had something to do with the crowd of people in the house. Obviously people made Dorothy nervous, afraid of something, but what?

"Oh, no, I don't mind a bit," she argued. "I love doing it. And it's so good for Judith to have people in. It gives her something to think about. She's enjoying herself. That's all that matters." She sighed suddenly, audibly. "I'm afraid we've been rather recluses since . . ." She stopped. "It must be very dull for Judith," she added with a distant look in her eyes. For a moment the listening expression was there, then she seemed to shake herself mentally. "Oh, well. I'd better set the table in the dining-room."

Before Sharon could offer to do it she

had glided away and Sharon was left to get on with the other preparations.

She was standing by the table, deftly arranging savoury eggs into a bowl of lettuce when Brent came into the room with a tray of dirty glasses. As if they had been merely an excuse to visit the kitchen he put them down on the bench.

"Oh, there you are," he said.

Immediately the supper was forgotten. They were alone and she was responsive, waiting for whatever he would say or do. She studied his face; his eyes were narrow and intense, his expression set.

"It's a lovely party, Brent," she ventured when he did not speak.

"I noticed that you were enjoying yourself," he answered, bitterly.

"What do you mean?"

"You know what I mean. You're having yourself quite a time with Cole."

"Oh, don't be silly. I wasn't having a time with him. *He* was having a time with *me*. You must know what he's like."

"Yes, I do. And I don't like it."

This was almost a declaration of jealousy at least and she held her breath. Was he going to say at last that he loved her? Oh,

Brent, she cried, silently, say it, please say it.

She moved towards him, her eyes wide and full of appeal, almost in a trance.

"Brent," she whispered, and, suddenly, they were close together in each other's arms. "Oh, Brent, Brent," she murmured against his mouth. "Oh, darling, you do love me, you do." She leaned her weight against him, her head against his shoulder. "Please, Brent, tell me that you love me."

His arms were tight around her and held her as though he protected her from something.

"If I do, will you trust me and go away from here? Go home and wait for me, until . . ."

"Until what?"

"Nothing. Will you go, just leave here?"

"But I can't do that, Brent. I feel that if I leave you now, something will happen. I'm afraid Brent, I'm afraid of what will happen to us. If I go away I'll lose you. I can feel it. Please, please tell me what it is you're afraid of."

There was a sudden surge of noise and people in the hall outside the door and they drew quickly apart, each trying to compose their features as a bunch of determined helpers came out to the kitchen with Dorothy. As the room filled up, Brent excused himself and went. She was caught up in the group of people and yearned to follow him. She felt horribly deflated, frustrated.

They served the supper in the dining-room and twenty or so people were not a crush by any means. But they were enough to prevent her seeking Brent out. How long would it be before they could be alone again? And so many people made the room hot. Sharon could not eat though the table looked colourful and the food delicious, mute tribute to Aunt Dorothy's powers as a cook. After a while she slipped out of the room through the reception hall and on to the front porch.

Faint white moonlight blanketed the garden. In the dark beneath the trees she could just discern the outline of Butch's kennel with the dog asleep outside it. Slowly she moved down the steps and on to the lawn. She stood in the shadows and gazed up at the top storey of the house. The new paint on the balcony gleamed.

She was unaware of Cole descending the

steps and moving across the lawn towards her until his shadow fell across her face. She jumped visibly.

"Oh, I didn't hear you coming . . ." She looked at him with trepidation, hoping he was not going to be difficult.

"Waal," he drawled. "You came outside after all."

"It was hot in there."

"Yeah. I told you."

He advanced towards her with an unmistakable look in his eye. "Ain't I lucky?" he said.

She backed away from him. "Now, Cole, keep away from me. If you touch me I'll scream. I will . . ."

"You won't scream. You're not the screaming type . . ."

"You'll find out . . ."

His hands reached out for her and she was imprisoned and she did not scream. She struggled and fought furiously, protesting. His face was a cynical grin loomed above her. But then, abruptly, she was free and Cole was lying on the grass, twisted sideways. She was panting as she realized that Nick had appeared. Cole staggered to his feet, the back of his hand pressed against a bruised jaw where Nick had hit him, just as he had seen the heroes of his western films do many times. If he had been wearing guns, he would have reached for them.

"You keep away from her," Nick was saying between clenched teeth. "Don't you ever lay a hand on her again. You keep away from her, do you hear me?"

"I'll get you for that," Cole hissed in his best movie manner. For a moment he looked as if he might attack Nick, but apparently sized up his chances and moved away.

Sharon was silent for a moment. "Thank you, Nick," she said at last. "How did you happen to come just when I needed you?"

"I noticed you were missing, and then Cole. That was just about all I needed. Are you hurt?"

"No. No, I'm all right."

"It's time to go home, Sharon. Get away from here."

She was completely calm again, her fright had abated, and, suddenly the situation became ludicrous. She thought of Cole playing it straight and she was amused. But as a smile started on her mouth she looked up and caught an expression on Nick's face that killed the smile before it was ripe. He did not think the incident funny. He was in a deadly earnest. Oh, no, she thought, with sadness, no, don't complicate things any more than they already are by falling in love with me.

It was nearly three o'clock in the morning before the guests began to drift away and from the sea could be heard the faint chug of motors as the sea-craft left for the various homes. Only Nick was not going home that night but was to sleep on the *Louise*. He seemed reluctant to go and was the last to leave. Dorothy stood on the porch with Sharon and watched the departing guests, and, strangely, adopted Judith's matchmaking tendencies.

"You two say good night while I go and finish the clearing up," she said to Sharon and Nick. Rather self-consciously they were left alone.

"Will you be comfortable for the night?" she asked after a silence.

"Uhuh. I often sleep on the *Louise*. It's

you I'm worried about. I want you to promise me that you'll leave here tomorrow."

"Oh, Nick. Why does everyone want me to go?"

"Who else has suggested you go?"

"Brent."

"Brent?"

"Yes. He seems to think I'm in some kind of danger. Just like you."

"That makes it really urgent. He ought to know."

"But I can't go, Nick. I just can't. If I go I'll never see him again . . ." She stopped, silenced by the expression on his face and regretting the hasty words. After the scene in the garden she felt she had lost a confidant, for how could she frankly discuss her love for Brent with him now that she suspected that he loved her?

"I must stay just a little longer," she added, quietly. "I'll be all right. Who could have any reason for hurting me?"

She smiled at him to lighten his mood and, as he stood on the step below her, casually holding his guitar in one hand, a brooding expression on his face, she felt a warm fondness for him.

She watched him disappear into the night with swift, easy strides, and when he was out of sight, she suddenly felt alone and unprotected.

The house was in darkness other than a light on the stairs. The reception hall was gloomy and forbidding and for a moment she caught her breath as she saw the figure beneath the stairs. Then she laughed disdainfully at herself. Of course, the suit of armour. I'm being frightened by my own imagination, she told herself, wishing that someone had stayed up. But everyone had apparently gone to bed including Aunt Dorothy who probably thought she and Nick would be outside a long time saying good night and had decided that the tactful thing to do was go to bed.

She mounted the stairs slowly seeing menacing shapes in the dark recesses of the hall and the passages above. Outside in the garden the dog began to howl mournfully. She shuddered and wished that she was somewhere else. She thought of the *Louise* and it became a refuge, a safe haven, and she longed to be there.

Outside her bedroom door she paused almost afraid to go inside, but why she did not know. And in the silent gloom she was sure that she could hear someone inside. Her hand on the door handle, she stood petrified aware of someone breathing heavily on the other side of the door. I must go in she told herself because then, perhaps, I will *know*. But her trembling fingers would not turn the knob. And then she could not hear the breathing and she wondered if, after all, she had imagined it. Boldly she turned the handle and stood on the threshold of the dark room. Her eyes darted about but she could see no one. But her gaze was held by the open french doors with the balcony beyond. The heavy curtains stirred in a sluggish breeze. Had she left the doors open? She could not remember. But whoever had been in the room was probably on the balcony. She did not waste any more time in being afraid. She sped across the room and out through the double doors and collided with Dorothy.

Unaware for a moment of who it was she fell back against the wall.

"Oh," she said. "It's you." She glanced quickly up and down the balcony and wondered if it was her imagination that made her see one of the far doors closing softly to.

"Can you hear it?" Aunt Dorothy asked in a hoarse whisper.

"Miss Warden," Sharon beseeched urgently. "Who came out of my room. Who was on the balcony with you?" But Dorothy's eyes held a distant expression, in her trance-like state she was miles away.

Sharon wanted to plead with her, to try to understand what was behind the fear in her eyes, but now she was too tired. She was physically and emotionally spent and she longed for her bed and oblivion. Everywhere she turned, it seemed, she came up against a brick wall and for tonight anyway she had had enough. As the family usually did she led Dorothy gently back to her own room and saw her into bed. She fell asleep almost immediately and Sharon was free to go to her room.

She closed the french doors securely and wished that she had a key to lock them but if one existed she did not know of it. There was a key in the lock of the door into the hall and she was glad to turn it and bolt her door against the night and the rest of the house. But she was afraid to go to bed with the balcony doors merely shut. What if the intruder should come back? For she was sure there had been an intruder.

She began to undress and moved across the room to turn down the covers. Her feet rooted themselves to the spot, her eyes dilated and she gasped aloud. There was a square of white paper on the pillow slip. With fingers that would not stop trembling she lifted it up and, by the light of the table lamp beside the bed, forced herself to concentrate on the few brief lines of printing on the paper.

If you value your life, go home.
Leave Warden's Cove.

11

SHE was shocked into a kind of numbness, and she was incredulous. Somehow despite the warnings and the prickings of her own instincts she had not really believed that anyone at Warden's Cove would do her any harm; she had tried not to believe that Margaret had been murdered.

Perhaps it was a joke this melodramatic note. She read it over and over. But who would play a joke like that on her? And why?

Which hand had written the note? The words were printed in large, clear letters, without characteristics. Perhaps someone in the family would recognise the printing, but who could she ask? She could not be sure that she was not asking the very person who had written it. She was unfamiliar with the handwriting of them all, even of Brent.

She could not possibly go to sleep, tired as she had been. The unlocked door on to the balcony would add to her terrors. She wanted to talk, to discuss this development, and there was no one in the house with whom she could talk. But there was Nick on the *Louise*. Would he mind being woken up at this time in the morning? She did not think so.

Hastily she pulled on her shoes and the frock she had only just taken off. With the note still in her hand she turned the door handle and slipped out into the passage. The light above the stairs gleamed fitfully, throwing shadows on the walls. And, now, she was afraid of the house, in each shaded corner there lurked danger; the house was suddenly more menacing. Perhaps the person who had written the note was abroad in the night, watching to see how she would react. In the cave beneath the stairs perhaps? She began to descend the stairs slowly, gripping the banister with one hand. She kept her eyes averted from the suit of armour afraid that it might suggest a person lying in wait.

The front door was unlocked and she slipped out into the night. On the path in the tree-shaded garden she felt impelled to look back at the brooding monster of a house. Her heart faltered as she thought she glimpsed a figure at the lounge window, partly concealed by the voluminous curtains. She moved down the garden path, feeling eyes boring into her back, jumping at shadows, sure that she was being pursued. It was a long, long way across the paddocks to the beach. She forced herself to hurry, almost running, afraid to look back, and, for a minute, she wished that she had stayed in her room and remained in bed, note or no note. She was panting as she arrived on the beach. A slight wind sighed over a calm sea, the moon teetered on the horizon, almost ready to vanish as dawn approached. And there was the *Louise*, with, miraculously, a light still burning in the cabin.

Her high heels clicked on the jetty as she made her way to the side of the boat. She was awkwardly climbing into the cockpit when Nick opened the cabin door to see who his visitor was.

"Sharon!" he said. "What the devil are you doing here?" He helped her into the boat and led her into the cabin. His hands gripped her shoulders. "Are you all right?"

She leaned against him weakly. For a moment, her confidence deserted her. "Oh, Nick," she murmured. "Someone was watching me."

He led her to the unmade bunk and she sat down, seeing that he was still fully dressed and that the other bunk was undisturbed. He had not, apparently, been to bed.

He sat down beside her, giving her all his attention.

"Who was watching you?"

"I don't know. Someone was watching me through the lounge window as I came away from the house. I thought they were following me."

"Let's get back to the beginning. Why did you come away from the house?"

She held out the scrap of paper. He looked at it for a moment, then took it and read it slowly. His expression did not change.

"I found this on my pillow," she said, slowly. "You know these people. Can you tell who wrote it? Do you recognize the printing?"

"I'm afraid not. Whoever wrote it made sure of that." He took one of her hands in his. "But this makes one thing for sure. You've got to get out of that place."

She was too shaken to argue. "But why would anyone threaten me like that? What have I done?"

"Asked too many questions p'raps."

"But I didn't. Not to start with. Everybody just told me things. I wasn't suspicious. Not at first. Everyone else was suspicious. Why should anyone mind what I think? You said yourself that there's been a lot of talk about Margaret's death and I don't know anything more than anyone else."

"But if you are staying on the property it might give you opportunities that casual friends and neighbours don't have."

"But I'm only here for a few days. I can't do much harm. And Judith asked me to stay. That wipes her out, doesn't it? I mean it couldn't be Judith who wrote the note."

"It could be. She might be trying to frighten you away from Brent."

She thought about this for a while. "No," she said at last. "I don't think it was Judith." She wanted to remind him of how Judith delighted in throwing them

174

together, but it was impossible to point this out to him. It would never satisfy Judith to just frighten her out of the house. Judith was a realist. She wanted Brent more securely than that and more surely.

"Brent himself might have written the note," he suggested levelly. "If he has something to hide about the death of his wife."

"No," she protested. "It doesn't sound like Brent. Brent is too mature. He wouldn't write childish notes." She stopped. It was too ominous to be childish.

"Then who do you suggest?"

"I don't know. I just don't know who would do such a thing. There's Cole," she added, reluctantly. "He might hate me after what happened tonight, but I don't think so. I mean . . . he wouldn't want me to leave if he's hoping to seduce me, would he?"

He smiled wryly. "I suppose not. Thinking of Cole naturally brings me round to Hank. Now he might be a possibility. He doesn't miss anything. Those eyes of his are taking everything in. I'd be willing to bet he can see what's going on between you and Cole and he wouldn't like Cole not getting his own way."

"But it seems so childish, and would a man who's been through what he's been through be so childish?"

"Why not? He doesn't seem to me to have a particularly high IQ. We can't wipe them all off. It's got to be somebody. If we wipe Hank, there's only Dorothy Warden."

Sharon thought about Dorothy Warden and her fly-away hair, her spinsterish-shyness and her kind, nervous manner. She did not seem a likely candidate.

"She was out on the balcony when I ran out to see who had been in my room," she admitted.

"Isn't that suspicious?"

"I didn't think so at the time. She was listening you see. She wasn't acting. She was almost in a trance. When I got as far as my bedroom door I could hear someone inside. Whoever it was was breathing heavily on the other side of the door. When I finally dared to open the door the room was empty and the doors on to the balcony were wide open. I went out on to the balcony and thought I saw someone disappear into a room further along."

"Whose room was it?"

"I don't know. I was too worked up to take it in properly. I suppose I should have checked. I might have only imagined it."

In the snug cabin and the security of his presence, she was calm again and wished she had followed the phantom figure if she had indeed seen one. She thought about Dorothy Warden again.

"Miss Warden might want me to go for Judith's sake. She sets great store by Judith's happiness. But she must see that Judith's been persuading me to stay." Her eyes grew thoughtful. "You know I do think this has got something to do with Margaret's death. I think she was murdered and that the person who did it is threatening me."

"The one person we can be sure knows the truth about Margaret's death, is Judith. If Margaret was murdered, either she did it or she's protecting someone else."

"But Judith couldn't have been in my room tonight. Aren't we forgetting that she's crippled? She can only move around with sticks with great difficulty. She wouldn't have had time to get out of my room tonight. No, there's only one way Judith could have written that note. If she had persuaded someone else to put it in my room."

"Dorothy Warden perhaps."

"Aunt Dorothy is her willing slave. She waits on her hand, foot and finger. She would do it if Judith asked her to, and she'd keep silent about it."

The battery-powered light in the cabin seemed to dim and the light from outside was growing stronger. Jolted Sharon realized that the dawn was breaking. She looked at her watch. It was nearly five o'clock.

"It's nearly daylight," she said.

"Mmm. It gets light early at this time of the year."

"I must go back before anyone wakes up."

"I'll be pulling out about ten o'clock. D'you think you can pack your bag and make a decent exit by then?"

She stood up and moved away from him. Now that it was nearly day time, her fears had abated, and she was again reluctant to leave Warden's Cove and probably lose Brent forever. I didn't come all the way here, chase him quite unashamedly, without pride, just to leave him because someone is threatening me, she told herself. I knew there was something very wrong to make Brent disappear the way he did, and just because I'm right, doesn't alter anything. I must stay and find out what it is.

"I . . . I don't think I'll leave today," she began cautiously.

He was standing in front of her; his long fingers gripped her shoulder, his eyebrows were pulled together in a frown.

"Hey, wait a minute. Now, don't let's get into an argument about that again. You're not crazy enough to stay here after this." He thrust the scrap of paper towards her. She could see that he was really angry. It's none of your business, she wanted to cry. I can do what I like. But she knew she could never say it. She could never hurt him in the face of his tremendous concern for her.

So she tried to be reasonable. "I'll just wait a day or two, Nick. Whoever wrote the note won't do anything for a day or two, surely. Anyway, if there is a murderer at Warden's Cove, or a potential murderer, wouldn't it be the right thing to do, to wait and unmask whoever it is?"

"Not at the risk of your life."

"I won't risk my life. I'll . . . I'll make it clear that I'm going home in a day or two. I'll set my time for departure. That should make it safe for me. I'll see that they all get the message. If the person knows that I'm leaving any day . . ."

"Anything can happen in a couple of days," he interrupted her. "I think we should show this bit of paper to the police and let them handle it."

She was shocked. "Oh, *no!* I couldn't do that. Brent would hate me. He'd never forgive me."

"It's the natural thing to do. Why should Brent care—unless he's got something to hide?"

"I know what you mean and I don't believe it's anything to do with him. But it would incriminate someone else in his family. It would all be so unpleasant . . ."

"It would be unpleasant to be killed by one of them."

"But if I stirred up a hornet's nest like

that . . ." She could imagine Brent's cool anger. "And it might just turn out to be a joke that . . . Cole . . . has thought up, to pay me out for rejecting his advances."

"Cole doesn't make jokes. He has absolutely no sense of humour."

He was right of course, but she would not be put off. Her life-time chance of happiness was at stake and she was determined to fight for it. But, apparently, he was just as determined that she should not stay.

"Sharon, get this straight. I'm not leaving here today without you. That's for sure. You can make up your mind to come quietly or I'll take you away by force."

She smiled weakly and he added, "I mean that, Sharon. I'll give you till ten o'clock and then I'm coming up to the house to take you away. I warn you, I'll make a scene if I have to, but I'm not going back to Te Kiri and leaving you in that mess."

"That's ridiculous."

"That's how it is."

She wanted to argue further, but she hesitated. Any more argument and she might say something she would regret, something that would make him declare himself in love with her and that she felt she could not face. There was nothing to do but hope that he did not mean it or that he would be too naturally reticent at the last minute to do it.

His manner changed as though he had declared his intentions and now there was nothing to do but wait. He relaxed. "Let's have a cup of coffee before you go back," he said.

12

SHE slipped into the house again when dawn was a reality. After the party of the night before she expected the family to sleep late and she wondered if there was time for an hour or two in bed before they awoke and the day officially began. Quietly she let herself into her room and began, again, to undress. But she did not feel tired and knew that she would not sleep. Over her lawn and nylon-lace slip she pulled a quilted dressing-gown. With care she creamed the make-up off her face, the light dusting of powder and pale lipstick that had been a concession to interest Brent.

Strong sunlight forced itself between a gap in the curtains across the door and after a while she pulled them back to expose the glass doors. She gasped, caught in surprise. Brent was on the balcony, standing back against the railing watching her room. Through the glass they looked at each other. He was fully dressed and she tried to understand what this might mean.

Slowly, she moved forward and opened wide the doors.

"Good morning," she murmured. "Another lovely day."

"So, you are back," he said, his face set in morose lines.

She controlled a start of surprise with difficulty.

"Back?"

"From Kane's boat. Where did you think I meant? You've been down in that blasted boat with him for more than two hours."

"I . . . I had something I wanted to . . . to tell him."

"And last night you spent the whole night with him in that isolated bay. All very innocent."

Her heart was thumping in an uncomfortable manner, she was weak with indignation and a strange sort of happiness that he cared what she was doing.

"I don't have to answer to you about what I do," she said at last. "I'm not . . . married . . . to you. You've gone to great pains to prove that as far as you're concerned I'm just an unwelcome guest in your home."

He turned away and looked over the railing towards the sea. While she watched silently, he ran his hand through his brown hair and appeared to be fighting some emotional battle. His taut body relaxed in almost a resigned attitude. She could not know or guess what private battle he waged, but she waited, tense, aware that it was important to her.

She was astounded when he turned and faced her and asked her, quietly, "Sharon will you marry me?"

"Brent!" She could find no other words.

"I mean it. Will you?"

"But I . . ."

"Do you want time to think it over?"

"No. I mean . . . it's not that . . . it's . . ."

"What?"

"Oh, Brent. I've wanted desperately to hear you say those words. I'm in love with you, you know that. I can't even hide it."

"I'm in love with you, Sharon." The wonderful, magic words. For a moment she was spellbound but, when he made no effort to touch her, she moved towards him and tentatively raised her hand to touch his cheek.

"Oh, Brent, I love you and I do want to marry you. More than anything else in the world. But something is wrong. What is it? You're so unhappy. Something is so very wrong . . ."

For a moment, his arms went round her and he held her gently against him, without passion, then cupped her face in his hands and studied her with searching gaze.

"No, nothing is wrong. You have made it right. You've no idea what your presence in this house means to me. You're like sunshine illuminating the dark corners, like fresh air dispelling the mustiness. Look at you now. Not a vestige of make-up . . . Everything about you is so natural. You smile more than anyone I've ever known. And it's a beautiful smile, full of kindness and concern for other people . . ."

They were the words of a man in love and, when he kissed her, she knew that the world should explode in a shower of fireworks to register her happiness, but something was missing. He was too resigned, almost desperate.

She waited for him to end the embrace, afraid to move lest the whole thing dissolve into a dream, until a sound behind them caught their attention. They drew slowly apart and turned to face Judith.

She was standing on the balcony just a few steps away, outside her own bedroom door, supporting herself with two short sticks. Sharon looked for hate and indignation on her face after what she had witnessed, but there were none. She looked very, very pathetic, her eyes were hollows of sadness. Instinctively they both moved protectingly towards her as though they feared she would fall. She drew back sharply.

"Don't touch me," she said.

They stopped, their hands held limply at their sides.

"I'm sorry, Judith," Sharon began.

"Sharon and I are going to be married," Brent told her, stiffly.

She paled visibly and again they feared she would fall. Sharon could feel only sympathy for her at that moment. Judith did not speak at all. She turned slowly and began to make her way painfully inside again.

Involuntarily Sharon stepped forward again, her hand outstretched. "Can't I help you?"

"No, thank you. I can manage on my own."

They did not see her again until the family met for breakfast on the terrace on the back lawn. She was sitting beside the table in her wheelchair wearing a red dress that was wonderful with her colouring. Her long arms were bare and the frock was cut low enough to expose her beautiful shoulders and neck. Sharon wondered how Brent could resist her. She was composed again and, as she spooned fruit into her breakfast dish and the household were grouped about the table, she asked, "And have you all been told that Brent and Sharon are to be married?"

There was an astonished silence. Sharon was acutely uncomfortable. She and Brent had planned to tell the assembled gathering this piece of news, but Judith's question was unexpected. Aunt Dorothy was sitting directly opposite Sharon and her hand jumped visibly so that her fruit spoon clicked against her plate. Her hand shook as she looked at Judith.

"Married?" she repeated, flustered.

Nonchalantly Judith lifted her spoon to her perfectly shaped mouth. "Yes. Isn't that nice?"

If Cole was surprised, he did not show it.

"Waal, just fancy that," he drawled; and Hank was mute, expressionless.

"Does that mean you're goin' to be my mother?" Danny demanded, his spoon poised, his eyes wide with surprise.

Sharon laughed lightly. "I'll do my best. Does that sound very awful, the prospect of having me for a mother?"

He thought this over so long that she was positively embarrassed. "No," he agreed at length. "You'll be okay."

She laughed again with relief. "Thank you. For a moment there I thought I wasn't going to make the grade."

With forced brightness Dorothy Warden stood up and moved round the table to Sharon who was standing beside the tea-pot ready to pour the tea.

"Well, that's lovely, my dear. I'm so glad for you both. Yes, it's just lovely."

But her eyes did not smile. She stood on tiptoe to kiss Brent.

"Brent, dear, my best wishes. I hope you'll both be very happy." She moved abruptly and turned her head away and they were all aware of the rush of tears to her eyes. "Yes, very, very happy," she persisted.

Sharon watched her in an agony of remorse. How dreadful that she and Brent should have to take their happiness at other people's expense. For Dorothy Warden would never be happy about it. She loved Judith too much. There were so many problems to be faced. What would happen when they were married and she lived here permanently? How could she possibly fit into this household where Judith made her home and suffered unrequited love for Brent, and where there was Cole to be contended with. And how could she usurp Dorothy's place in the household and become its mistress?

There followed a long, uncomfortable silence as each person tried to show interest only in their breakfasts. Sharon was glad when the meal was over and the men drifted away. Brent, Sharon thought,

190

seemed relieved to go, making an excuse that he had some accounts to attend to in the office, the pokey room reserved for this purpose off the hall upstairs. Eventually only the three women were left and Sharon began to help Dorothy with the clearing up. Judith remained in her chair, her hands idle in her lap, her face in repose, apparently deep in thought. While Dorothy Warden went on with the washing up, Sharon went back and forth to the house clearing the table. She found the silent Judith disconcerting and, each time she appeared on the terrace, she cast her an anxious glance. At last Judith gave her her attention.

"So, you are going to marry Brent." There was no expression in her voice.

"I'm sorry Judith."

"You needn't be. You're not married yet."

"That . . . that sounds like a threat."

"It's a warning, shall we say. Don't be misled by Brent, Sharon. He's not in love with you. He loves me and it will be me he marries."

Sharon did not reply. She avoided Judith's eyes and carried the last remains of the meal away. She could not argue with Judith. For one thing Judith was at such a disadvantage when Brent had just proposed to Sharon; and at such a pathetic disadvantage being in a wheelchair. All Sharon's best arguments were ones she could not use. But deep inside she knew she did not want to discuss it further with Judith for other reasons. She did not like Judith's assurance that Brent loved her.

She thought about it while she helped Dorothy with the dishes. Could Judith have been threatening her? Was it Judith who had written the note and then used the crisis to remind her of it?

There was another crisis coming up, she knew, and, when she looked at her watch and found that it was nine o'clock, she realized that she would have to go down to the beach and forestall Nick. She could not possibly have him hauling her away from here now.

About nine-fifteen she set off down the drive towards the beach. It was another lovely day with a cloudless sky and a calm sea. As she emerged through the gate and started across the burnt-brown paddocks she could see Danny and the dog gambolling on the sand.

"Hi!"

She turned, startled in a reverie. Cole was approaching on his horse with his shadow in the background.

"Hi," she murmured. Then, "Hello, Hank." She could not use his name without an ironic twist, but this slight sarcasm was apparently lost on them both. Or perhaps not on Hank himself. Past Cole, she found herself looking into the dark, quiet face. What was he thinking about? She could hardly remember him speaking one word in the time she had been on the property, his dark, brooding presence seemed always in evidence.

Cole dismounted and stood by his horse, holding him lightly by the bridle.

"So you're goin' to git married to Brent," he began.

"Yes, that's right." She watched him warily.

"That's what you think." His eyes narrowed, he leered at her, nodding his head in a thoughtful manner. "Yeah, that's what you think."

"I don't *think*, I *know* I am."

"You're kiddin' yourself. Brent won't marry you. He'll marry Judith. He's in love with Judith, he's been in love with her for years."

She had not yet recovered from her encounter with Judith and to hear Cole use almost the same words, was too much. She felt sick with apprehension.

"Brent is suffering from—what d'you call it?—a guilt complex. I'm not up on these fancy words, but I know what that means."

"I don't understand you."

"He feels guilty because he killed Margaret. He thinks he hates Judith 'cause he did it for her. And you're somebody different, from outside. You didn't have anything to do with the whole mess . . ."

For Cole, Sharon considered, this showed remarkable insight. It even sounded truthful. But she would not believe that Brent did not love her. She thought of the scene on the balcony that morning, but this reminded her of his despair and the words he had spoken. She thrust them from her for they seemed to support Cole's theory. You are like sunshine and fresh air, Brent had said.

And she could not believe that Brent had killed his wife.

"Brent did not kill Margaret. You don't know anything about it. You don't even live in the house . . ."

"We slept in the house then, Hank and me. We only moved out to the bunkhouse afterwards. We were on the balcony just after Margaret fell or got pushed. As I told the cops, Brent was already there. Soon as we heard Margaret scream we rushed out in our pyjamas, but Brent was there already—and dressed. As I told the cops."

Her voice was heavy with sarcasm and bitter anger. "You tried to incriminate your own brother with the police. You wanted them to think he had killed his wife; you hate him so much. And you want me to believe it, but I won't either. And thank goodness the police were intelligent enough to see through you."

"It ain't all finished yet," said Cole.

He mounted the horse again and jerked the animal's head around in the other direction. She wanted to call after them as they trotted off, to force this discussion through to a conclusion, but she would not let him think she believed him. With a heavy heart she started off again towards the beach, her thoughts in a turmoil. Cole's dislike and contempt for his brother were so naked. Would he carry it as far as killing Margaret, or persuading Hank to kill Margaret, with a view to pinning the murder on Brent? She thrust the thought away. It was too fantastic. But anything at all was beginning to seem possible at Warden's Cove.

As she neared the beach she noticed that Nick had joined the boy and the dog on the sand. Probably waiting until ten o'clock, filling in time, she surmised. A look of relief lit his face for a moment when he saw her, but it disappeared when he realized that she did not have a suitcase.

"You've come," he said. "But where's your bag?"

She looked around for Danny. He and the dog were paddling at the fringe of the waves.

"Now, Nick," she began. "I can't come with you. I can't possibly come. Everything is different now." She took a deep, sharp breath as though preparing herself for the next sentence. "Brent has . . . asked me to marry him."

He could not hide his startled reaction. "He's what?"

"He asked me to marry him." She smiled ruefully. "Don't act so surprised. It's not very flattering." He was silent and she went on, "I know what you're going to say. That he's in love with Judith. That everybody knows he's in love with Judith."

"No, I wasn't going to say that."

"But, you're thinking it."

"I'm not thinking anything except that you must get out of here. Despite anything Brent has done, someone's threatening you. Have you forgotten that?"

"No, I've not forgotten. But I'm willing to risk it. I've got to."

"That's ridiculous."

Unbidden, her eyes filled with sudden tears. She did not easily cry and she surprised even herself. She shook her head to shake them away. "I'm being very silly," she said. "But, please, Nick, please don't make a scene. Just leave me. Don't you see, this is the one chance I've got. I'm in love with him, Nick. If I leave something will take him off me."

For a long time he was silent. His

expression, when he did speak, was curiously resigned. "Okay. Why don't you tell me to mind my own business?"

"Oh, Nick . . ."

"If you need me . . . if anything . . . frightens you . . . you must promise to ring me up. I'll be at the pub or, if I'm not, they'll know where to find me. The number is 159K. Got that?"

She nodded. "I'll be all right."

"This damned place is so isolated and I don't do the run again until Tuesday. And I don't have a show of getting here much under an hour and a half."

"Nothing will happen, Nick. Brent is here."

He did not look reassured. "Lock your door at night and try to keep in a group. Don't be alone with any of them, not even for a few minutes. There's safety in numbers."

She watched him wave good-bye to Danny and go along the jetty. She stood as though turned to stone while he untied the *Louise*. For a moment, he stood uncertainly on the jetty looking her way, then he saluted her with his hand, climbed into the cockpit and started the engine.

Slowly the *Louise* drew away from the wharf while Danny waved from the beach. I should stop him, she told herself. I should go with him. I'm frightened to be here without him. But she stood unmoving.

Only when the boat had chugged her way round the first line of cliffs and could be seen no more, did she turn back towards the forbidding structure of the homestead.

At lunch-time she was really afraid.

She had set the table for Dorothy for a full three-course luncheon and they had all partaken of the soup course and the soup dishes had been removed to the kitchen. Sharon carried the leg of lamb from the kitchen and placed it at the head of the table for Brent to carve.

"Where's the carving knife?" he asked, searching around the plate without finding it.

Aunt Dorothy hovered at his elbow. "Oh, yes, the carving knife." She fluttered into the house and appeared again without the knife.

"I don't seem to be able to find it," she

said. "Has anybody seen the carving knife?"

No one answered. Sharon looked around the ring of faces.

"Never mind," Brent said, quietly "The old one will do."

"But Brent." Aunt Dorothy was upset "You like to use the one that matches the set . . ."

"It doesn't matter," he persisted patiently. "We'll look for it later."

Aunt Dorothy went for the substitute Everyone waited with varying degrees o patience for their second course. It was a simple enough incident. Aunt Dorothy was just the sort of person who migh mislay a knife. She was silly to let i trouble her, Sharon told herself. No one else was perturbed. She looked around the impenetrable faces. And she was terribly afraid.

13

AFTER the midday meal the family, tired after the very late night, retired to their various rooms for a rest. Sharon, who had not slept at all the night before, was glad to lie down for a while. She removed her frock and her shoes and lay in her slip on top of the bed. It was almost too hot to sleep but she was desperately tired. She lay awake waiting for sleep to come. I must sleep now, she told herself. I must sleep in the daylight. I think I'm going to be too afraid to sleep tonight.

But was it safe to sleep in the daylight? She had drawn the curtains across the glass doors and the room was shadowed, but she was terribly conscious that the doors were not locked. All the bedrooms opened off the balcony, and anyone in the house could quite easily slip into her room. And perhaps they would choose this very time when all the household rested. She got up again and moved a chair. With difficulty she jammed its back under the double-door handles. At least she would be awakened by the noise should anyone attempt to enter the room.

But she could not sleep. Each time she dozed it seemed she heard footsteps on the balcony and woke again with a start, her heart thumping hugely, her breath coming with difficulty. Her eyes dilated she lay tense until she could be sure that it was only her imagination and that no one lurked outside. After an hour of these fitful snatches of sleep she suddenly slept heavily for more than two hours and woke to find that her wristlet watch showed the time at after four o'clock.

She listened intently for a while. There was no sound of people moving around on the top floor but she thought she could hear a hum of voices in the dining-room which was almost beneath her bedroom. She could imagine them all grouped about the room waiting perhaps for Dorothy Warden to make coffee.

It took her only a few minutes to dress, comb her hair and apply a little fresh lipstick. Swiftly, she put the room in order, removing the chair from under the door catches, pulling aside the heavy curtains.

As she descended the stairs she realized that there were indeed voices to be heard in the dining-room. One, a strange voice, new to her, rose and fell above the rest. She paused on the stairs and listened, wondering who it could be. It was a man she could hear, but it was a light-textured voice capable of low, penetrating laughter; laughter that chilled her, left her with an almost psychic sense of foreboding.

He was a young man, thin and dark, with permanent creases down his cheeks as though he laughed often. But his eyes held no laughter.

When Sharon appeared Dorothy, Judith and Brent were all in the room with the stranger. He was standing in front of the fireplace, leaning nonchalantly against the mantelpiece, one hand stuffed into the pocket of his trousers, and wearing an open-necked white shirt.

"Oh, you've woken up," Dorothy greeted her. "I'm just going to make coffee. I'm afraid we all overslept. We were so tired after last night."

The man was watching her through

narrowed eyes and Brent introduced him briefly. "You don't know my brother-in-law, do you, Sharon? George Paxton. He's Judith's brother and has just descended on us." There was a distinct coolness, an open dislike in Brent's tone. "This is Sharon Denholm. Miss Denholm and I are going to be married." The words were clipped, almost bitter.

"Is that so?" George turned to his sister. "That's one in the eye for you, Sis."

Judith's sweet face tightened with anger and she looked pointedly away. Sharon burnt with sympathy for her.

She looked about the room. They were all tense. Quite obviously he was very unwelcome.

"That will do, George," Brent snapped. "Now that you're here I suggest that you tell us why."

George shrugged and laughed briefly.

"I came to pay you a visit. I haven't been near you for a year or more."

"No."

"Don't you want to know where the black sheep has been?"

"Not particularly."

"Well, the black sheep wants to tell you

204

where he's been. I've been round the world on a freighter. I only just got back."

Brent was cynical. "We heard you had a manager on your place."

"I was away when Margaret was killed. I only heard about it when I got back."

"We didn't know where you were. We couldn't notify you."

"Gave me quite a shock it did." His eyes were narrow and intense for a moment, then, suddenly he laughed in an insinuating manner. "Yes, gave me quite a shock."

"It gave us a shock too," Brent agreed ironically. "All right, George, let's finish with this clowning. What do you want?"

"Want?"

"Yes, you've come here for something. What is it?"

George laughed again and stuffed both hands in his pockets. "What do I want? What do I always want? Money, Brent, money. I happen to be broke. That piece of dirt I own doesn't bring me in enough to live on. Sure I had somebody on it while I was away, but that ate up all the income. I'd sell it if I could find a buyer but who would live on this God-forsaken strip of coast? Now it's different for you. How many thousand acres 've you got?" Brent did not answer and he went on, "Yes, I need money, Brent. I need money."

"And what makes you think you'll get any from me?"

The laugh rang out and was cut sharply.

"I think I will, Brent. I think I will."

"I don't think you will," Brent countered.

He laughed again as though he were amused by some tremendous private joke. "It will be interesting to see who's right, won't it?"

Judith moved her wheelchair slightly so that she faced him.

"You are not welcome here, George. And I suggest you leave."

"I will when I'm ready," he told her bluntly.

"You'll go when we are ready," she argued. "This is our home."

"I won't impose on your hospitality," he told her with sarcasm. "I intend to live on my boat. Or perhaps the three-mile limit applies in these waters."

Dorothy came in at that minute with the

afternoon tea trolley and the argument lapsed, but the air of strain remained.

Even Danny was apparently wary of this uncle for afterwards he came into the kitchen where Sharon was drying the dishes for Dorothy Warden.

"Did you see my Uncle George?" he asked her.

"Mmm. Yes, I saw him."

"He's a bad type, Uncle George."

"Danny!" Dorothy exclaimed. "You mustn't talk about your Uncle like that." She twisted round from the sink to look at him where he had perched himself on the table.

"It's true. You know it's true, Aunt Dorothy. Dad says so. Aunt Judith says so. Everybody says so."

He sounded rather proud of his uncle.

"You shouldn't listen to adults' conversation," his aunt reprimanded him. "Sometimes grown-ups . . . well. They don't understand each other . . . and they say things that perhaps they don't really mean . . ." Dorothy was obviously upset and Sharon liked her for it. She was old-fashioned enough to see a gap between children and adults and to believe it wrong when the adults' world intruded into the child's. She was protective towards the whole family and did not like to have Danny know that his father had spoken like that about his uncle.

When Danny had gone again, she apparently felt the need to justify Brent and Judith to Sharon.

"Don't think too badly of Brent and Judith," she said. "Danny's an only child on the place and he hears a lot of things it would be best he didn't. But there's no other company for him but adults and you can't be shooing him out of the room all the time or he'd have no company at all. We've rather got in the habit of talking in front of him a bit much."

"I can see how it must be."

"And George is rather trying at times. He used to come here a lot when Margaret . . . before Margaret . . . died. They were alike; George and Margaret. Judith's the odd one out in that family. George is a . . . scoundrel . . . I'm afraid. He's always trying to get something out of Brent. Oh, dear. He thinks Brent's made of money. He only comes here when he wants something."

Which was kind, old-fashioned Dorothy's way of saying that George was a cadger, a no-hoper, Sharon decided, translating it into up-to-date language. And he was dangerous. When she thought of George she, too, felt protective about the family at Warden's Cove.

He did not appear the rest of the day but they were all aware that he was down at the water's edge, lying low in his boat which turned out to be rather like Nick's. It was anchored in the bay and as evening approached and the daylight decreased, a light could be seen in the cabin.

As the daylight waned Sharon found herself growing more and more tense. Soon it would be time to leave the brightly lit lounge and climb the dark stairs to her room. She felt weary for the afternoon sleep had not refreshed her and she longed to creep into bed and sleep peacefully until the morning. But, tired as she was, she knew she could not let herself sleep that night. Whoever had written the note might be abroad. She looked across at Brent who was sitting in an armchair opposite her glancing through a two-days'-old newspaper which was the newest one they had. She wished desperately that she could tell him about the note, and she wondered why she could not. Was it because she did not trust him, that she was afraid he might have written it?

Aunt Dorothy chatted lightly, trying to be entertaining, but Judith was preoccupied. She was one of the few people Sharon had known who could sit absolutely still, her hands in her lap, unoccupied, apparently deep in thought.

After a while she looked across at Brent and murmured, "Brent."

He did not look up. "Yes?"

"What are we going to do about George?"

He folded the paper slowly without looking at her.

"I can't see that there's anything we can do. I believe he has a legal right to anchor out in the bay if he wants to."

"But he intends to make trouble."

"What trouble can he make?"

"What trouble could he ever make? But he always did. He . . . he acted so oddly . . . as if he had something up his sleeve . . ."

Brent stood up. "Don't worry about him. I can cope with George. I always have."

"You look tired, Brent," Dorothy interrupted incongruously. "Don't sit up with us. Go to bed if you want to." She stood up, too. "As a matter of fact I feel all-in. I think it would be a good idea if we all got an early night."

The little group broke up. Dorothy went ahead upstairs to put the light on in Judith's room and have ready the wheelchair which was kept there. Sharon followed her reluctantly. She wanted to talk to Brent, she wanted to be alone with him. She stood with Dorothy on the landing watching him carry Judith up the long flight. Since his return he did it each night for her, naturally and with ease. Perhaps it was the thought of the future when Sharon would be mistress in the house that prompted Dorothy to explain again, "We've been talking of getting a lift put in so that Judith can get up and down stairs on her own. We've written to the contractors but we're so out of the way they haven't come yet."

Sharon did not answer. She was

watching the expression on Judith's face that was so close to Brent's own and her heart ached. There was something so right and proper about Brent and Judith as a team that she felt like an outsider. She turned away from the luminous, unconcealed devotion on Judith's face.

To hide her confusion she went into Judith's room to fetch the wheelchair. She stood just inside the door trying to control a nausea in the pit of her stomach. Dorothy fluttered in and began turning the bed down, laying out Judith's nightdress. Sharon busied herself with the wheelchair and steered it into the passage.

Brent and Judith were at the top of the stairs apparently unaware of her presence so wrapped up in each other they were. There was an expression on Brent's face as he looked at Judith that Sharon had never seen before. Suddenly both Judith's arms were around his neck, she pulled his head down to hers and kissed him for a long time on the mouth.

"Brent, oh, Brent."

Sharon moved back into the room lest they see her. She waited a long time before she moved back into the corridor. When she did she surprised them just outside the door. Judith's arms were still about Brent's neck and she was whispering urgently to him.

"Brent, what does he want? What is it he knows that makes him so sure of himself?"

The whisper died as she became aware of Sharon. Brent lowered her into the chair. They said good night and left her with Dorothy.

Brent would have gone to his room but Sharon detained him. She felt there were things she just had to say to him. She could not bear his casual approach a minute longer.

"Brent, I must talk to you."

He hesitated. "Yes?"

Her eyes were full of appeal, begging him to be kind. "There are so many things to be said. I mean . . . if we are to be married . . ."

"We can talk about it some other time." He did not look or sound like a man in love, at least not a man in love with *her*, Sharon thought.

"But I want to talk about it now, Brent. I . . . I feel you've been avoiding being alone with me all day. But this morning you asked me to marry you, remember? Naturally I want to make plans . . . Perhaps it's different for you. I mean you've already been married once, but this is new to me. And . . . I'm a girl and it's a big moment in my life . . ."

His face softened as if he were seeing her properly for the first time and understanding her anxieties.

"Very well. Where would you like to . . . talk?"

She indicated her room and moved towards the door. "Shall we go in here?"

She preceded him into the room and sat down on one of the two chairs inside. She was terribly tense but she tried to breathe deeply to calm herself, quite unaware that she appeared, to him, like a courageous schoolgirl determined to be brave and face an unpleasant issue. There was something touching about her confusion, and he waited patiently for her to begin.

"What is it you want to know?" he asked after a long silence.

"I . . . I would like to make a date for our wedding for one thing."

He looked away. "There's no desperate hurry, is there?"

She bit her lip. "I suppose not. But I'm expected home by the end of this next week and I would like to know when it is to be."

He shrugged. "It doesn't matter much when."

"You . . . you don't sound . . . very impatient . . ." Her face coloured as she said it. That morning he had been desperately anxious to make her his wife, but now he sounded almost as if he regretted the proposal. She began to wish that she had not forced the issue. It would have been better to wait and let him make the decisions. But there was so little time. And she was sure he was hiding things from her.

"Naturally I don't want to wait too long," he agreed at last. "But there are so many things to be done. Don't you want time to organize it properly; a white wedding dress and all the trimmings."

"I suppose so." But she was only half-hearted. She knew she did not care about her wedding dress or any of these usual trimmings. She just wanted to be married to him; quickly before he was lost to her.

"What about May or June?"

She wanted to protest that May and June were many months away, but she bit the words back. She had already humiliated herself enough. She nodded briefly.

"What else do you want to talk about?"

But she could not answer because she did not know what it was she wanted so earnestly to discuss. Deep inside she knew that she wanted to be reassured that he loved her, to have everything cut and dried and explained so that she could relax and go home and make plans for their lives together.

"I suppose we'll live here when we're married?"

"Of course. Where else?"

"And . . . and Judith will still be here . . . ?"

"Of course. She has lived here since she was a child. This is her home."

"Yes, but, Brent, you and Judith . . ."

"What about Judith and me?" There was a wary look on his face and she was frightened.

"Nothing."

Suddenly his attention was diverted. A concentrated frown appeared on his face. He stood up and moved across to the double doors. He was listening and she forgot their conversation and listened, too.

"Shsh," he said. "There's somebody out in the garden."

She felt a little chill creep over her. He pushed the doors open and moved out on to the balcony. She followed him quietly.

A full moon bathed the garden in yellow, dull light. Below them Butch stirred outside his kennel. They stood on the balcony and looked down. Together they became aware of the shadowy figure of a man standing beneath the trees. His face was a white triangle turned up towards them.

Impulsively Sharon reached out and touched Brent's arm. "Who is it?" she whispered.

The figure laughed suddenly; a quiet menacing laugh.

"Oh, it's him."

"What are you doing down there, George?" Brent demanded. Beneath Sharon's fingers his muscles were tense.

"Did I give you two lovebirds a fright?" The laugh again.

"Get off this property, George. You're trespassing."

"I was just imagining Margaret falling from up there. Just exactly where you're standing I should say."

Sharon withdrew her free hand from the railing with a start, but Brent kept calm.

"Get out of here."

"That must have been quite a night," George went on. "Yes, that must have been quite a night." He waved his hand nonchalantly. "Have fun." He disappeared into the shadows of the trees. They watched for him on the drive but it was too dark to see if he had really left the garden and gone back to his boat. Once they both heard, quite plainly, another long, low laugh, but it seemed a long way off.

They went back into the bedroom. Sharon found she was shaking. There was something about George that frightened her terribly.

"Brent, what does he want? Please, please tell me who he is."

"He's Margaret and Judith's brother," he answered tightly.

"But there's more to it than that. Why is he acting like this? Please, don't keep anything from me."

"I don't know any more than you do. We've never hit it off. That's all I know."

He had withdrawn into himself and she knew that any intimacy they had shared was lost.

"Go to bed now," he said and kissed her briefly on the forehead. "I'm exhausted and you must be, too. Forget about George. He won't be back."

But she could not believe him. She could not even be sure that George had moved out of the garden.

14

SHE could not prevent herself from dozing lightly. With a chair fitted under the door handles she lay on the bed fully clothed. Just to rest, she told herself. I won't go to sleep. I mustn't. But every few minutes it seemed she would jerk violently, become wide awake and realize that she had dozed off. Waves of sleep washed over her. Sometimes she got up and moved about the room to keep herself awake and on the defensive. Towards morning her urgent need of rest would not be denied and she fell into a heavy slumber. She awoke with a start as daylight lightened the room. She was shaking and, strangely, she felt cold. Her fingers were clenched into fists. She lay still staring at the ceiling afraid to move, sensing a danger in the room. After a long time, she willed herself to look around. The furniture loomed, ghostly in the half-light. There was no one there. Then her eyes focused on the double doors and her heart lurched sickeningly. The doors were slightly open.

She sat up and put her feet on the floor. The chair lay on its side on the carpet.

"Oh . . ." She shuddered with horror to think that she had slept so soundly that she had not heard someone break into her room. She was weak with tension. But she was safe. No one had attempted to harm her. Unsteadily, she stood up and moved across to right the chair. Who had been in the room while she slept? She opened the doors and moved out on to the balcony. It was empty and silent in the early morning light.

She went inside again and along to the bathroom. While the house slept she took a bath and dressed in a fresh frock. She stood at the dressing-table in the bedroom, moving her face this way and that, studying it for best effect. She combed her hair into neat order experimentally pushing it high on her head the way Kerry wore hers, but it would not stay in place without hair spray and she did not possess any. For the first time in her life she was taking an interest in her appearance other than to feel tidy and clean. The feminine adjunct that she had always felt rather contemptuous of, suddenly assumed an importance. She thought of Judith's cool perfection and sighed to think she must compete with it. Apparently men like sophistication, the correct make-up, the newest hair style. She thought of Nick. With him she had felt free to be entirely natural. Her hair had hung casually about her face, perhaps even untidily, and she had not worried about whether or not there was any lipstick left on her mouth. But I'm not in love with him, she told herself. It's different for Brent. But how did she know what Brent liked when he concealed his real self from her, hiding behind some secret she could not share?

She went through the sleeping house, down the stairs, which were not half so frightening in the daylight, and through the hall to the back door. It opened easily. She had noticed that it was never locked. And why should anyone lock the door of a property like this when only the immediate family and Hank lived on the place. And George, she added silently. The stranger who had entered her bedroom could have been any one of them.

Early morning light filtered through the garden, birds were chirping in the heavy trees. She was startled to see a figure at work on the flower-beds, alongside the concrete path. Dorothy Warden, oblivious to her, kneeling with a trowel in one hand and wearing, although it was so early, a large, shady sun hat.

"Miss Warden," she said. "What are you doing out here at this hour?"

Dorothy turned blue, startled eyes upon her.

"Oh, you gave me quite a turn." She twisted the trowel in the grey earth. "I'm doing a bit of gardening. I often get out early in the morning before anyone's about. I get so little time for it during the day."

"Let me help."

"Goodness, no! You'll get all dirty. And you've got a good frock on too."

"I'll be careful of it." She lifted the frock above her knees and knelt down on the spongy grass. With the help of a gardening fork that was on hand she began to weed a patch. It was lovely in the beautiful garden at the beginning of a new day. She paused and lifted her head to listen to the birds. What a delightful place this was to live. How happy she would be if she could live here forever as Brent's wife.

"Miss Warden," she began thoughtfully after a comradely silence. "I wonder . . . Have you found the carving knife?"

Dorothy turned and smiled briefly. "Yes. Wasn't it silly of me? I had wrapped it up with some potato peelings. I don't know how I did it. It must have been on the bench when I did the potatoes. I was so worried about that knife. I just thought of every place I could. I was so glad when I found it."

"I'm glad you did." So she had been unnecessarily afraid, at least of the knife; jumping at shadows.

After a while Sharon asked her another question. "Miss Warden . . . what does George want?"

Dorothy stood up and pulled off her gardening gloves before she answered.

"I'd better get in and start the breakfast."

Sharon stood up too. "What does George want?"

They looked at each other in silence.

There was a vague expression in Dorothy's eyes.

"I don't know. But he'll make trouble. George always makes trouble. He'll tell us what his threats mean when the time suits him."

And she was right for when they were all at breakfast on the patio that morning, the time apparently suited him. They heard his voice first, calling. "Where is everybody?" And, it seemed that everyone tensed, that the atmosphere changed subtly.

"God!" Cole exclaimed. "Is that damn critter still here?"

The critter appeared round the side of the house and made his way along the path to where they waited silently.

"So you're all here," he said and the insinuating laugh escaped him.

No one replied for a moment. Then, Judith, her voice cold answered, "Yes, we are. And I suggest that you tell us what you're doing here and what it is you want."

He acknowledged her with a sneer and a nod of his head in her direction. "That's just what I'm going to do, Sis. That's just what I'm going to do. You know what I want. Money. I've already put my cards on the table. I want money." He looked at Brent. "If I don't get it I'm going to have to try a nasty little bit of blackmail." He laughed again without mirth.

Sharon looked round the faces. She felt she was on the verge of a discovery, something that would help her solve the mystery of Margaret's death, and she waited with bated breath. Did this strange brother of Judith's known something about it? That it was something to do with Margaret she did not doubt.

Brent stood up, his face tight, etched with lines of anger. "I don't know what you're talking about, George, but I've ordered you off the place before. Now get out before I throw you out."

George held his hand out in front of him as though to ward Brent off. "Now, now, Brent. Don't start being the big shot with me. I *know* things about you." His palm relaxed, flicked into his trouser pocket and came out grasping a slip of paper. "When you see this I think you'll change your mind."

The expressions on the faces did not

change. He looked around waiting for a reaction but there was none.

"So, you don't recognize it, eh?" In a moment he was smoothing the scrap out on the table. "Shall I read out what's written on it? That'll interest you." He surveyed them slowly. "Someone here, isn't going to like this." He enunciated clearly as he read the words on the paper. "If you value your life, give Brent his freedom."

It was fantastic. The only person who reacted to this recitation was Sharon. Her surprised gasp made them all turn to look at her. She stared back until his voice went on and they listened to him again. "That note was written to Margaret not long before she died. You want to see it?" He picked it up and passed it to Brent. "Someone here wrote that note and left it in Margaret's room. And not long after, she died."

Brent held the note in two hands and studied it quietly, displaying no emotion. Sharon moved closer to read it. It was incredible. The printing and the wording were so much like the note she had found on her bed. She shuddered. Someone had written Margaret this note and she had died not long afterwards and the same someone had written her a similiar note.

"This doesn't mean a thing," Brent said calmly. "I don't recognize the writing." He handed it back towards George and added, contemptuously. "You probably wrote it yourself."

Equally calm, George took the note back. "This was sent to me by Margaret a few days before she died, and you can act as innocent as you like. I've got the letter that came with it to prove it. She wrote to me for help, but she didn't know I was off round the world. This only caught up with me when I got back. Somebody was threatening Margaret and somebody pushed her off that balcony. Now that somebody has got to pay or else."

"Or else what?" Brent asked in a dangerously quiet voice.

"The police would be interested in this." George held the paper aloft and before the others realized what was happening Cole had plucked it out of his hand and torn it into small pieces.

"So much for that," Cole sneered.

But George was unperturbed. "You

think that's the only one? She got two or three similar ones and I've got the others. And the letter. You think I'd come here with all the evidence?"

Cole's smirk of triumph faded and Sharon felt quite sorry for him.

"No one is going to pay you a cent, George. You can go to the police," Brent said and Sharon ached with love for him. "Now get off this property."

George laughed sardonically. "Okay, okay." His laugh faded and he looked around the group. "One of you knows something about this letter and whoever it is'd better see me before I leave here 'cause when I go it'll be to the police."

They watched him leave. Sharon expected an animated discussion to break out when he was out of sight. Surely Brent —someone—would probe, would want to solve the mystery of the note. But no one did. They were all silent as though each one had something to hide and did not want the matter discussed.

But Sharon wanted to know more. She had to know who had written the notes to Margaret and the note to her. She wanted to run after George, call him back, ask him questions. He knew the family well and must be familiar with their handwriting. And Margaret. She must have had some idea who was sending her the notes. She would have told him in the letter. It became terribly urgent to talk to George alone. But how could she talk to George? She had no excuse that the family knew of for seeking him out. She searched their faces again, striving to see some guilt. Someone here knew that she, too, had a letter, but who was it?

She would have to go down to the beach and talk to him. But that was impossible because it would entail an explanation she could not make. The only way she could see him unobserved would be to go down at night when everyone had retired to bed. Yes, that was what she would have to do.

But, after all, she did not have to wait for the night. For later that morning when she was in the garden helping Dorothy to finish the patch they had worked on earlier, she had a premonition, a feeling that they were being watched. Dorothy went on working placidly, but Sharon glanced uneasily around and there he was, several yards away standing among the trees, watching them. How silently he moved about. He seemed to be almost invisible. In broad daylight he had made his way into the garden from the beach without apparently being seen. For a moment he remained standing there, then he turned and disappeared into the trees.

With only a murmured apology, a slight excuse, she left Dorothy and followed the path round the house. But as soon as she was out of Dorothy's sight, she doubled back into the patch of trees where she had seen him. She moved swiftly and, as she drew near to the path and the garden wall, she saw him again. He was standing just within the shelter of the trees as though he waited an opportunity to leave the garden unobserved.

"Mr. Paxton," she called, quietly.

He turned round. "Look who's here."

"I want to talk to you, Mr. Paxton. I must ask you some questions about the letter and those notes."

"You know who wrote the notes?"

"No, no, I don't. But you must have some idea. There must have been something in the letter. Margaret must have had some idea who would do it."

He was watching her through veiled eyes. "What's it to you?" he asked.

She ignored the question. "Why didn't Margaret call the police if she was being threatened?"

He relaxed a little and shrugged. "People don't always. Why rattle all the family skeletons? She had her reasons."

This seemed reasonable to Sharon. After all, she, too, was being threatened, but she had not called the police. There was too much at stake. And, perhaps, for Margaret, there had been too much at stake; her marriage, her position in the household. A thing like that could have too many repercussions and certainly be very unpleasant.

"That note suggests that Margaret was murdered so that Brent could be free to marry . . . Judith." She made herself say it.

"He always had his eye on Judith."

The words twisted a knife in her heart but she went on, "Who would want him to be free?"

"Brent and Judith, who else?"

"Then it must have been Judith who did it. She was there."

But her reason argued. It needed not be either of them. Dorothy loved Judith enough to desire her happiness above all else. Cole hated Brent enough to attempt a murder if he thought Brent would be blamed for it. The notes did not prove anything except perhaps the motive.

"Who did Margaret think had written the notes?" she begged him. "She knew all their handwriting. Even if it was disguised, she might have known."

"She thought it was Brent," he said.

Her head whirled. The blood seemed to rush away from her brain and leave her shocked. Then, into the dreadful silence, a gun barked. The sound reached them just a second ahead of the bullet which skimmed between their heads and bedded in a tree trunk behind them. Like one person they flung themselves behind the tree for protection. They waited but there were no more shots. After a while Sharon moved to look about for their attacker but she could not tell from whence the shot had come. The garden lay quiet in bright sunshine. Over the nearby garden wall the gently sloping paddocks appeared to be empty.

"Somebody tried to kill me," George said in disbelief.

Who could it have been? There were guns all over the Warden homestead she had noticed. Hank and Cole sometimes toted a gun in their work. She had heard someone say they saw an occasional rabbit but she had suspected that Cole just liked to play cowboys with it; it made him feel more like the genuine article. But Cole and Hank were good riflemen, it was unlikely that either would have missed the target.

"Somebody, damn them, tried to kill me," George repeated, and laughed through a mirthless mouth.

But had he been the target? It might have been meant for me, she told herself, frightened.

15

SHE tried to tell Brent about it afterwards. She wanted to see his reaction, to be assured that he had not fired the gun. "She thought it was Brent," George Paxton had said.

She found him in his office working at the desk on some accounts. Obviously he did not want to be disturbed. He was frowning as he turned to listen to her and she knew he was concealing his irritaton with difficulty.

She tried to keep calm and describe the scene without emotion. "Someone tried to kill me, Brent," she finished up. "Someone tried to kill me, or George Paxton."

"May I ask what you were doing with George Paxton?" His tone was cold.

She was shocked that his first concern was not that someone had attempted to take her life; he did not even seem surprised.

"I just happened to see him in the

garden. I . . . I asked him about the notes . . ."

"The notes?"

"I wanted to know who wrote them, Brent."

"I told George to keep off this place. If he sets foot on the property again, I'll take a gun to him myself."

The conversation was getting out of hand. She was appalled that he was not taking her story seriously.

"Brent, someone tried to kill me. Don't you understand? Someone deliberately shot at me."

"That's ridiculous. Who would do that? You probably heard Cole or Hank shooting at a rabbit."

She found her anger mounting, and she controlled her temper with difficulty. "The bullet hit the tree between us, Brent. I can show it to you. It's still lodged in the bark. Oh, you must admit that this all adds up to something. The notes George Paxton has, and this attempt on his or my life. Somebody wrote those notes and somebody tried to kill one of us, and for the same purpose . . ."

"What do you mean by that?"

236

"It's . . . it's something to do with you. Oh, Brent, don't pretend to misunderstand me. Margaret was threatened because she was married to you and wouldn't give you a divorce."

His face paled with anger and she wished she had not said it.

"Who told you that?" He was icy and she was a little afraid of him.

"Everybody tells me that . . . that you wanted Margaret to divorce you but that she wouldn't. The note spoke for itself. You didn't seem . . . surprised at what was in the note."

"Do you think I was going to let George Paxton think he had surprised me? I'm not taking those notes of his seriously. They were a practical joke, or something he's thought up since to get money out of us."

She thought of the note she had of her own and was tempted to tell him about it. Surely he would find that convincing. She could not understand just why she did not tell him of it. Was it because she did not quite trust him?

"But he has a letter of Margaret's to prove it," she argued. "At least he says he has."

"And I don't doubt that, invited to do so, he would produce the letter. Margaret may even have written the notes herself."

"Why would she do that?"

"Why? Why do you always want to know why? She did things like that. She was vindictive. She might have thought she could hurt me some way by writing the notes. My wife was an epileptic. I suppose some of those damn people who can't mind their own business have told you that?"

"Yes."

"She could be very sweet and gentle for long periods, but she had strange moods when it was impossible to understand her. Often she was sorry afterwards, but she kept us all on edge. We didn't know quite what to expect of her."

"And, Brent, do you really think she fell off the balcony?"

"Of course."

"Just a short time ago you wanted me to leave because you said it might be dangerous for me here."

"Dangerous?"

They were interrupted just as he repeated the word by Dorothy Warden.

She came along the hall, her hair flying, calling in her thin soprano voice for Sharon.

"You are wanted on the telephone."

"The telephone?"

"Yes. Someone in Te Kiri."

"The reception is very bad and I couldn't catch who they said was calling."

Brent lifted the receiver from the telephone on his desk. "Take it here," he offered.

Reluctantly she accepted the receiver and held it to her ear.

"Hello. This is Sharon Denholm."

"Hello." Quite obviously it was Nick's voice and she wondered how Dorothy could not have known.

"Oh . . . Nick." The next moment, as Brent lifted his head, she wished she had not used his name.

The wire crackled and his voice seemed a long way off. "Are you all right?"

"Yes . . . of course . . ."

"I know it must be hard for you to talk. Is anyone with you?"

"Yes."

"Then I can't ask you any questions. I just wanted to check that . . . that nothing had happened. Do you want to get out of that place? I could fetch you in less than two hours."

"No, no of course not."

"You know the phone number if you change your mind?"

"Yes."

It occurred to her that Dorothy could quite easily have lifted the receiver downstairs to check that they were connected before hanging it up and that she could be a listener to this conversation, even if accidentally.

"Thank you for ringing. I really must go now," she told him, agitated. She replaced the receiver hastily. Brent's head was bent over the books on the desk, but his knuckles gripping the pen were white. She wanted to explain why Nick should ring her up, but there was no explanation she could make. And Brent obviously expected her to say something about it. For a moment she was furious with Nick for interrupting their conversation, though unwittingly, and for putting her in such a position. But the irritation was only momentary. It was replaced with warm gratitude that he was worried about her safety. In comparison Brent seemed so cold and unfeeling. For the first time her love for him wavered. She looked down at his bent head and it did not stir her to tenderness. He had asked her to be his wife and yet he would not discuss his affairs with her. He had put her in a position where her life was in danger and he would not tell her what he knew or explain the strange circumstances of his wife's death. If she were wise she would ask Nick to fetch her, would leave Warden's Cove forever and build a life apart from Brent Warden. She had a sudden vision of the hotel in Te Kiri, the laughter and the noise, Nick with his guitar! Nick who was safety.

She was here in this strange house with this man who declared he loved her but of whom she was afraid. Her life was in danger. These people were strangers to her. She did not even know who her enemy was—or if she had any friends among them. And she was tired from last night, and must soon face another night without sleep.

She thought briefly of ringing the hotel back and asking Nick to fetch her, but, almost as if he had read her thoughts, Brent suddenly relaxed and reached for her hand.

"You must forgive me if I seem terse," he said, quietly. "I've had a lot on my mind since Margaret died. And this idea that's just sprung up out of nowhere that she was murdered is the last straw."

He stood up and she went gladly into his arms. "Oh, Brent. Oh, darling," she murmured, immediately weak with affection again.

But Dorothy was coming back along the hall calling Brent this time.

"Doctor Matthews is here, Brent."

She turned and went back downstairs. Sharon looked at Brent in surprise.

"He comes in to ask after Aunt Dorothy," he explained. "He makes a trip along the coast to see old Mrs. Benson from time to time. She's crippled with arthritis. And when he does he calls in here. He's been treating Aunt Dorothy ever since . . . since Margaret died. But he says there's nothing much can be done. We've got to wait until something unlocks her memory."

She went with him downstairs, frustrated that their moment of intimacy had been interrupted before they had reached an understanding.

The doctor was in the living-room, standing in front of the fireplace as if he were quite used to being there, talking to Judith. Brent introduced Sharon briefly, adding, "Sharon and I are to be married, Alan. You can talk in front of her."

The stocky, middle-aged doctor, murmured an acknowledgment of the introduction, and shook Brent's hand.

"Congratulations. I had no idea . . ." The sentence seemed to fall apart in mid-air. As though his eyes were pulled by a magnet, the doctor looked at Judith, but she was studiously looking elsewhere. Really, Sharon thought, it was ludicrous the way everybody considered Judith's reaction to her engagement.

Brent went across to the heavy, mahogany sideboard and poured drinks for them all. He handed them round on a serving tray.

"Nice of you to come in, Alan," he said as he proffered him a glass.

"And how is Dorothy?" the doctor asked him.

"She's just the same." Brent glanced round to see that Dorothy had not entered the room while his back was turned. "She's perfectly normal most of the time. But at least six times since you were here she's been found on the balcony late at night, listening for something. God knows what it is. We just put her back to bed and she falls asleep quite naturally. Afterwards she doesn't seem to remember what happened—or that anything happened at all."

"No. She's like two people," the doctor explained. "One person exists in ordinary, everyday life, and the other exists in these trances. She suffered a shock the night Margaret died. When someone or something reminds her of what it was she'll probably revert to normal. In the meantime the two existences are separate. When she's normal she doesn't know anything about the trances, or the listening. She's living two lives and we've got to wait for an overlap. Someday something will remind her of what happened that night and her world of reality and fantasy will fall into place and become one."

Sharon listened quietly, trying hard to

understand it for did not Dorothy possess a clue to the mystery of Margaret's death and Brent's behaviour. There was a question nagging in her mind, demanding to be asked though she knew it was probably unwise to ask it here in front of this audience. But, perhaps, she would never get another chance. She avoided looking at Brent as she asked it.

"Doctor, you examined Mrs. Warden . . . after . . . after her death, I suppose. Could you tell if she had had an epileptic fit that might have caused her to fall?"

She was aware of Brent's unconcealed anger and Judith's rigid attention. Her fists clenched unintentionally and she concentrated on the doctor. He did not seem surprised by the question, and unaware of the tension.

"That's not an easy question to answer," he said, quite jovially. "It took so long for me to get here. She had been . . . dead some time. There were signs of a recent epileptic fit, yes. But she had taken such a turn earlier that day. Isn't that right, Brent?"

"Yes." The reply was terse.

Sharon did not dare press the issue

further. She knew Brent was furious with her. She had taken advantage of the doctor's apparently long-standing friendship with the family to pry into the affair. And Doctor Matthews, accepting her as Brent's future wife with only his welfare at heart and having been told by Brent that he could talk freely to her, had responded to her questions. But did she have Brent's welfare at heart? Would she probe for the truth of Margaret's death if she had, when deep inside she knew that she still suspected he might be the murderer?

16

"WOULDN'T you like to come for a swim in the creek?" Danny asked her as she sat in the garden after lunch trying hard to write a convincing letter to her parents. She could just imagine them worrying about her and the rather secret life she was leading. They would be glad when her holiday was over and she was safely back home, going each day to the bank.

She smiled at Danny. He was wearing a tee-shirt and khaki shorts, his white-blond hair was ruffled and he had no shoes on. She thought of the trip by horse over the jagged paddocks and the idea did not appeal. Anyway, there was this letter to be written. She must have it ready for Nick to take into Te Kiri in the morning.

"I might go into the bush and look for birds," Danny added. "If you keep very quiet, you'll see hundreds."

That, she thought, might be fun, for she loved the outdoors, but she could not spare the time. The days were passing and soon she must go home perhaps with the mystery of Margaret's death still unsolved, still with the dreadful uncertainty of Brent's affection hanging over her. There must be a climax soon. Time was too important to spend at the creek or even bird-watching in the bush.

"I'm sorry, I just can't," she told Danny. "I've got things to do this afternoon. How about some other time?"

He was not hurt by her refusal but went off quite happily with the dog at his heels and a few minutes later she could see him at a distance riding his horse across the nearest paddocks.

She went on with the letter. I'll try to be home at the end of the week, she wrote. The end of the week. Something would have to happen before then. She wondered why she did not tell her mother that she was engaged, and if it was because she did not feel that she really was. She could not be certain that she would ever be Brent's wife while he was subject to his strange moods, and while his wife's death was unexplained.

She thought about the morning and the

gunshot. How could Brent have been so casual about it—surely not unless he had fired it or knew who did? Could it have been Cole or Hank shooting at a rabbit? She was sure it was not.

However, after she had finished the letter with great difficulty and it was safely sealed in its envelope, she set off across the paddocks towards the shepherd's cottage where Cole and Hank slept. As she drew near she could see the two of them on the veranda, being very leisurely for the hour of the day. They worked hard, she knew, but now they were lounging on the porch. Hank was idly strumming his guitar. "Meanwhile . . . back at the ranch . . ." she said to herself with irony.

Both men stood up as she approached and waited, Cole with his thumbs hooked in his belt.

"Well, look who's here," he said.

"Howdy," she said. "Oh, don't get up. I don't want to interrupt you."

Cole pushed a chair forward. "Why don't you sit down and join us?" He was watching her through narrowed eyes.

She sat down on the chair. They both waited as if for an explanation of this unlikely visit and she could not think of any way to be natural about it. She looked at a gun leaning against a veranda post. Yes, Hank and Cole were familiar with guns.

"I . . . I wondered if you were doing any shooting this morning?" She swept an appealing glance across their expressionless features. "I . . . I thought I heard a shot."

Cole shrugged. "Might've been us. We practise in the morning sometimes."

"This morning?"

Cole looked at Hank. "Were we practising this morning, Hank?" he asked deliberately.

Hank looked at them through veiled eyes. "Yeah."

"That's right so we were," Cole agreed.

Their attitude irritated Sharon. This was a matter of life and death and, she felt, they were being flippant. But there was a little wave of fear in her stomach for she was sure that they knew something about the shot. And probably that meant that one of them had written the note and, most frightening of all, killed Margaret. She stared at Cole for a long time. He was not a man she would like to cross swords

250

with. And he must already hate her for the humiliation he had suffered at Nick's hands on her behalf. Oh, why don't I just give up and go home? she thought.

Hate her? This unpredictable man had a surprise in store for her. He moved another hardbacked chair round to face her. He swung a long leg across the seat and sat on it as though it were a horse, his arms resting on the back. It did not deter him that Hank was an audience to his words.

"I've got a proposition to put to you," he said.

"Yes?"

"I'm a grown man now and I need a woman. I've decided to git married."

"Oh," she murmured startled but still not prepared for his next words.

"You're it. You'll do me."

She was speechless. The words took a moment to register and when they did she was almost overcome by the desire to give way to laughter. It was ludicrous. Surely the strangest proposal any girl ever had. She looked sideways at Hank, faintly pink with embarrassment that this should be happening in front of him. He was so obviously the more intelligent of the two. His expression was inscrutable. If he thought Cole slightly ridiculous, it did not show. His loyalty to Cole knew no bounds, she decided.

"Is that a proposal?" she asked, faintly.

"What else?"

"But . . . but you can't be serious?"

"Why not?"

"I'm engaged to Brent for one thing. You know that."

"D'ya reckon? That's just what you think. Judith'll get Brent. You wait and see. And when she does, you'll see it my way. I've got a nice little filly in training for you. It'll be my weddin' present. I can just see you in that saddle."

"Well, I can't," she retorted. She shook her head in amazement. "Why, on earth, would you want to marry me?"

"You look good on a horse," he said.

She laughed. "Oh, thank you."

He missed the sarcasm. "It would get me even with that fisherman critter," he added, incongruously. "I've got a score to settle with him."

She was horrified. "You mean you want

to marry me just to score off against Nick?"

"Nobody gets away with punching Cole Warden," he said, grimly. "And that guy's gone on you."

She was shocked by his egotistical, childish reasoning. So juvenile. And this was a man who played with guns! And she was frightened now for Nick.

Alarmed, she argued. "That's ridiculous. You can't possibly have anything against Nick. He did it for me."

"Say yes and I'll fergit the whole thing," he bribed.

"That's out of the question. I'm engaged to Brent."

He shrugged as if enough had been said about that. She was furious with him and she still did not know if he had fired the shot.

"Cole," she said deliberately, "someone fired a shot at me this morning, or at George Paxton."

"That buzzard," he said without showing any reaction.

"Someone wanted to kill one of us. George perhaps, because of the notes . . ."

"Good for somebody. Anybody who takes a pot at George is a pal of mine."

She was as irritated by him as she had been by Brent. Why did they take her revelation so lightly? Why did they all act as if they had something to hide?

"Oh, don't be so flippant," she cried in anger. "Someone was threatening Margaret Warden, and George Paxton is a threat to that person's security." She stood up and moved away from him staring across the paddocks to the bay where the launch was still anchored.

He watched her, thoughtfully. "Don't worry about that buzzard," he said after a while. "Hank and I c'n handle him."

She turned round abruptly. "What do you mean?"

"He won't be here for long, that's for sure. I'm fixin' to do a little blackmail of my own. That there launch won't be in sight by sundown."

"What are you talking about?"

"He'll put out this afternoon. You just watch. And it'll be the last we'll see of him."

"And how are you going to make him do that?"

"Just like I said. Hank'n I'll do a little blackmailing of our own. Two can play at that game. Either he shuts up about the notes or we put him in a spot."

"But . . . but what have you got against him?" She was bewildered by these wheels within wheels.

"E'rybody's got somethin' they want to hide. And George has been double-dealing all his life. Him and Margaret were thick as thieves and he used to write her things. Don't let it worry you. George will be taken care of . . ."

His voice was sinister. Her head reeled. There were so many questions demanding to be answered but she was afraid to ask him too much. Certainly he had just proposed to her but she was not sure that he would be above killing her. She was afraid to goad him too far.

But, later that afternoon, she was to remember his words for the launch did indeed pull out and disappear round the cliffs.

She had been sitting in the garden with Judith who, perched by the garden table in her wheelchair, was doing some mending. It was oppressively hot even in the shade of the trees. Sharon offered to help with the darning Judith was executing so carefully, but her offer had been brushed aside. They were Brent's and Danny's socks Judith was mending and she did it meticulously. As if she loved the owners, Sharon told herself unhappily.

After a while Brent wandered out.

"That office gets damned hot," he said. "I've been in there nearly all day and I've had enough." He looked about the garden for his son. "Where's Danny?"

Sharon told him. "He went for a swim in the creek. Why does he prefer the creek to the sea?" she asked as an afterthought.

Brent smiled slightly. She had seldom seen him smile and something constricted inside her when he did. "We make him shower when he goes in the sea, but the creek is fresh water."

Over the darning Judith was watching them silently and Sharon was horribly conscious of her gaze. How dreadful to take her own happiness and hurt someone else so much.

"Why don't you go for a swim before tea, Sharon?" Judith suggested, suddenly.

"It's so very hot. You would enjoy it. I can lend you a bathing suit."

She wants to be alone with Brent, Sharon told herself and was about to offer an excuse not to go when Brent suddenly added, "That's a good idea. I could use a dip myself. That's just what I need after the day in the office."

Judith's expression did not change not even when they both came downstairs again wearing their bathing suits under towelling jackets. Sharon felt terribly disturbed for her as they set off down the path to the beach. It seemed cruel of them to be displaying their physical fitness to her in this manner.

If things had been different the interlude would have made her very happy. Brent, apparently relaxed, had sought her company, had volunteered to go swimming with her just as any man in love might do. In the hot, sultry afternoon, the sea sparkled invitingly. She should have been happy, but she was not.

And there on the horizon was George Paxton's launch heading out of the bay just as Cole had said it would.

"Oh," she said, "he's going."

Brent's eyes narrowed against the sun. "George? So he is."

"Aren't you . . . surprised?"

"No. He knew he'd get no money out of me."

"But . . . but what about the notes?"

"He won't do anything about them—if he has any others. The police don't care for blackmailers. He could make it very unpleasant for himself, having tried a trick like that."

"I think Cole has frightened him off," she told him. "He told me he knew things about George that could get him into trouble with the police and that he was going to make a deal with him over the notes."

"He told you that?"

"Yes. He more or less said that George had written certain things to . . . to your wife . . . that he knew what was in her letters . . ."

"Cole should mind his own business," he snapped, abruptly, and she wished that she had not told him of Cole's plans. "I must go through my wife's papers. I've been putting it off."

She had spoiled his mood and she

changed the subject quickly, trying to recapture the happier moment.

"Isn't the sea glorious?"

She threw off her jacket and raced across the sand into the surf. He called after her but she took no notice. Better, she thought, to leave him alone for a few minutes until he relaxed. She was a strong swimmer and the sea was warm. She plunged through line after line of mild breakers until she was in deeper water. She swam with long, lazy strokes, enjoying the sun, the sea, the sky, the salty air. On the beach Brent pulled off his jacket and she saw him coming through the breakers towards her. She watched his tall, brown, spray-washed body. For the little physical labour he did he was in remarkable condition.

But, as he drew nearer, she saw that his expression was strange and intense. He was ploughing through the water towards her in a determined way, like a man with a mission, certainly not like a man enjoying a lazy, afternoon swim. She began to feel apprehensive and all sorts of doubts crowded into her mind. His sudden desire to go swimming with her had been out of character. What did she really know about this man? They were alone in this vastness of sea and sky, there were no witnesses.

He came nearer and nearer and all reason seemed to desert her. She could not be logical; she was wildly suspicious and afraid. Breathlessly, she turned and swam further away from him.

"Sharon. Sharon." She could hear him calling her name above the murmur of the waves. He was a powerful swimmer and she was weakened by irrational fear, and soon she could hear his loud breathing behind her and knew he was gaining. And then his strong hands reached for her and she struggled and tried to avoid him.

"You fool," he was saying. "You fool . . ."

She fought wildly, tried to scream; a wave washed across her open mouth, she felt as though she choked and for a moment her head was beneath the water. Threshing about she struggled back to the surface, fighting with all that was in her.

"You fool," he cried again. "You'll drown us both."

She grew weaker and, against her will,

she found she was being held in a life-saving grip and he was guiding her through the waves towards the shore. They were washed up onto the beach like seaweed and they lay exhausted panting on the beach just out of reach of the hungry breakers.

He lifted his head off the sand, his breath still coming in short gasps. "What got into you? What on earth did you think I was trying to do? Drown you?"

She turned her face away from him. "What *were* you trying to do?"

"Get you away from a dangerous spot. There's a nasty undertow that far out and some jagged rocks under the surface. You nearly killed us both."

"I'm sorry." Her apology was merely a murmur. Then she turned to face him. "Forgive me, Brent. It's just that I'm all on edge. This morning someone tried to kill me."

She sat up, shaking the water from her hair. He reached for a towel and rubbed his shoulders and body dry. She yearned towards him and wished that he would melt and take her in his arms.

"When are you going home?" he asked after a moment.

"Home?"

"Yes." His voice was deliberate. "I think it would be just as well if you went back home." He turned to face her and his face was distraught. "Just leave me to work all this out," he pleaded.

"All what?"

"You know what I mean, Sharon. Go home now and wait for me. I . . . I'll have less to worry about if you're not here."

As if he had said more than he intended to he stood up and reached for the towelling jacket.

"I'd better get back to the house."

He moved away from her, across the beach and she had to hurry to keep up with him. She looked sideways at his set face and knew that the moment of intimacy was over and he would say nothing more.

Judith was still in the garden when they arrived back at the house, and Sharon found herself avoiding her eyes. To hide her confusion she busied about helping Dorothy to set the table for tea and did not notice that Judith kept looking at her wristlet watch and was growing perturbed.

"What time is it?" she asked Sharon after a while, and held the watch to her ear as if she thought it might have stopped.

Sharon looked at her own watch. "Nearly half past five."

"I thought so. I wonder where Danny is? He should be home for tea by now. He knows five o'clock is the limit for stopping at the creek."

"He said he might go into the bush to look for birds," Sharon told her innocently and was not prepared for Judith's startled reaction.

"Into the bush? But it would be almost dark in the bush by now."

"He's probably got so interested in what he's doing that he's forgotten the time."

"But he could hardly see now. Have you seen the bush? It's absolutely untouched natural bush and so dense. Oh, I've asked Brent not to let him go in there. He could get lost so easily, but Brent says he knows it like the back of his hand."

At that moment Brent came back, casually dressed in slacks and a sports shirt.

"What's that?" he asked, hearing his name.

Judith turned to him eagerly, her expression worried, her fingers gripping the arms of her chair.

"Oh, Brent. Danny isn't home. And it's half-past five."

He was unperturbed. "He'll be here any minute. Boys don't always keep track of time."

"But Sharon says he's gone into the bush."

He thought that over for a moment and his eyes wandered to the horizon where the dark range of hills lay shrouded in dense undergrowth.

"He knows what he's doing. And he knows the bush."

"But he might have gone too far in," Judith argued desperately.

He looked at her in silence for a moment and there was something in his face that Sharon could not bear to see. He leaned towards Judith so that their heads were close together and laid one hand gently on her clenched fist.

"Don't worry about him." He was touched by her concern for his son. "If he doesn't get back in a few minutes I'll send Cole or Hank to fetch him."

Sharon busied herself with the table unable to bear the intimacy the two shared. This is how it must have been when Margaret was alive, she told herself. The thought shocked her. Now, it's me, not Margaret, she thought. No, no, I won't think like that, she hastily corrected herself. She was not a stumbling block to his happiness. He wanted to marry her, not Judith. If he loved and wanted Judith she was there, free. He could have taken her at any time since his wife's death.

"Please, send them now, Brent," Judith pleaded. "I feel that something has happened to Danny."

"All right. Just to put your mind at rest."

He went inside to telephone the cottage for one of the two men and the two women were left alone.

"You love Danny, don't you?" Sharon said at last.

There was no mistaking Judith's sincerity. "Of course. I was here when he was born. I've seen him grow from a baby to the boy he is now. I've looked after him when Margaret had . . . one of her turns . . ." Her voice was low. "I love him as if he were my own child."

Brent came back to say that Cole had gone to bring Danny home. The table was laid and Brent carved the cold roast to be eaten with lettuce salad. They made light conversation among themselves, but consciously they were all waiting.

"Cole's been gone a long time," Judith said at last.

Brent looked at his watch. "He'll be here in a minute."

They sat outside, grouped about the table, and waited. They wondered whether to move the meal indoors, but the light still remained—a lovely, summer evening.

Then Cole came back, alone.

"I don't seem to be able to find him," he said. "Hasn't he come back while I've been gone?"

There was an edge to Brent's voice. "No. There must be some signs of him. Where did you look?"

"Up and down the creek and through some of the nearest bush. His horse is wandering around out there, so I figured he might be back."

"His horse wasn't at the creek?"

"Nope. It must have got unhitched and made its way home. Don't know how I missed passing it, but when I got back just now there it was in the paddock close to the house."

"The dog," Judith interrupted. "Did you see the dog?"

"Not a sign."

She turned to Brent, despair in her face, and fear. "Oh, Brent . . ."

Brent did not waste any more time. "I think it's time we organized a proper search," he said, quietly. "Where's Hank?"

"Over at the bunkhouse cleanin' up," Cole told him. "He's waiting for me to git back before he comes over for tea."

"That will have to wait," Brent said. "Ask Hank to come with us and bring any torches you've got over there . . ."

Dorothy fluttered about asking if he would like a quick tea before they went but Brent brushed her off and Sharon could see that he was really worried.

Cole, passing Sharon as he left, leaned over to ask her, "You been thinkin' over what I said this afternoon?"

She looked startled, concerned as she was for Danny and having almost forgotten their earlier conversation.

"About you and me getting hitched," he added.

"I certainly haven't," she said.

"You think about it. You could do a lot worse'n me."

"That's what you think." She was angry with him and his apparent lack of concern for Danny. "How can you go on about that while Danny's missing? Aren't you at all worried about him?"

"Nope. That kid can look after himself. He's just strayed too far into the bush. We'll find him. Probably asleep waiting to be found. Ain't nothin' can hurt him in that bush. Just a few birds."

"There might be a . . . wild pig . . ."

"I wouldn't like to be any wild pig gittin' tangled up with Butch. Besides, like I said, Danny can look after himself. We'll find him in no time."

"You always know everything, don't you? You always have all the answers."

He apparently missed the sarcastic note in her voice.

"Sure do," he agreed.

When the men had gone the three women were left alone. Sharon would have liked to go too but, though she had offered to help, Brent had protested that there was nothing she could do. She knew this to be true, she was quite unused to native bush for one thing.

Dorothy Warden made tea and they sat at the table and tried to eat. The salad was delicious but they had no appetites. The hot tea was a comfort, however, and, in the way of women, they drank two or three cups each. The shadows lengthened. Each knew that it was time to move indoors but each waited hoping that the men would come back and the crisis be over.

When the meal could be prolonged no longer, Dorothy stood up and began to clear the table and they moved inside. Dorothy went back and forth carrying the dirty dishes while Sharon began the washing up and Judith the drying. She did it sitting in her chair just inside the kitchen door, calmly and methodically reaching for a plate, a saucer, from the bench and placing them dry on the table.

"It's clouding over," Sharon murmured

looking out of the window above the sink. "I hope it isn't going to rain."

"Rain? That would be terrible. It would make everything so difficult."

The casual remark worried Judith so much, Sharon wished she had not said it.

"I'm sure they'll be back any minute," she added, hastily.

Judith was silent for a moment and, then, surprisingly asked, "What did Cole have to say to you when he left?"

Sharon looked at her and Judith met her look with wide, frank, unflinching eyes. If that is a rude question the look seemed to say, I'm not sorry. I want to know.

"He . . . he asked me if I had thought over . . . something he had asked me this afternoon." Judith was silent. "He proposed to me this afternoon."

Judith made a sound of impatience. "Cole is a silly child."

Sharon smiled slightly. "That's not very flattering. You can't understand him wanting to marry me?"

"I can understand him wanting to marry you but not for the reason you think. I don't mean that you're unattractive. I can imagine you've had many men proposing to you. But Cole! He probably did it to score off against Brent."

This was so near the truth that Sharon was surprised into silence. Really. How penetrating they all were. How well they knew each other.

After a moment, she decided to tell Judith the truth.

"No, it was Nick he wanted to score against. He has some strange idea that Nick is . . . attracted to me."

"It isn't a strange idea. Anyone can see that. What has Cole got against Nick?"

"He . . . he defended me against Cole the night of the party. Cole tried to . . . to get fresh."

"And how did you answer Cole?"

"I told him not to be ridiculous, of course. He knows . . . I'm going to marry Brent."

She could not look at Judith as she said it. She was filled with a tremendous reluctance to hurt her further. But her marriage to Brent was a fact and Judith would have to learn to live with it. She waited for Judith to argue as she had done earlier, but she was silent. After a long pause, she moved across to wipe any crumbs from the table with the dishcloth, and they were face to face again.

"I . . . I want you to know that I'm . . . I'm sorry about that, Judith," Sharon said, quietly. "I don't want to hurt you. I wish everything was different."

For a moment Judith's defences were down, her confidence shattered. There were bright tears in her eyes though her head was held high.

"It does hurt me," she said, slowly. "I love Brent. What you feel for him is nothing compared to the love I have for him. It goes so far back. To when I was just a child and he gave me a home when he married Margaret. There's a wall between us now, but I'll get through it. Please, Sharon, please, give him up. Go away. He loves me. Give him time and it will all work out. I must just be patient."

At the same moment they both became aware of Dorothy standing in the doorway with the tablecloth in her hands, and the conversation lapsed. Judith turned her head away and briefly brushed her eyes with the back of her hand and Sharon went back to wiping the bench with great concentration.

"Have you finished? How quick you've been," Dorothy said with forced brightness. "It's very cloudy outside. I do hope it isn't going to rain. Oh, why, why don't they come back?"

And they began to wait again.

17

LATER they sat in the living-room. While Dorothy was out of the room for a few minutes Sharon contemplated re-opening the conversation that she had spoiled earlier, but Judith was remote again, sitting by the window with a far-away look in her eyes and Sharon was loath to upset her. Besides there was nothing to say. Judith had begged her to give Brent up, but that she had no intention of doing. I love him too much, she protested to herself.

It was very dark outside, a thick blanket of clouds obscured the moon. The room was lit only by the standard lamp in one corner. Sharon had a sudden wild desire to run through the house, switching on all the lights.

Alone in the house with the two women she felt unreasonably afraid and her ears strained to hear the sound of the men returning. She gave herself a good talking-to mentally to calm herself. Why should she be afraid with the men gone for after all she did not know who her adversary was! I'm probably safer now than I have been since I came here, she told herself, for surely Judith who was crippled and Dorothy who was so vague and kind would not deliberately do her any harm.

Her listening ears heard a sound, vague and distant, but not the sound of the men returning.

"What is that? Can you hear it?" she asked Judith.

Judith listened. "Hear that?"

"A . . . a sort of buzzing sound. Like a . . . a bee or a blow-fly in the room . . ."

"I can't hear anything . . ."

But, now, Sharon could not be sure that she heard anything either. She shook herself. She was letting her imagination run away with her. This listening business was catchy. It came from being with Dorothy too much.

"Perhaps I'm imagining it," she admitted, but it seemed that faint and far away the sound persisted.

She sat down on one of the hard-backed chairs and clenched her hands in her lap, wondering what Brent was doing at that moment and seeing him in her mind in the dark and tangled undergrowth.

"How long will they be?" It seemed that Judith asked herself the question.

"Surely not long now. Would you like me to make you some coffee? Is there anything I can do for you?"

The standard lamp highlighted the blue in Judith's dark hair and accentuated the pale colour of her skin.

"Could you go outside and see if there's any sign of them? If you looked over the back-garden fence you could see them coming across the paddocks a long way off."

Sharon wanted to protest that she was afraid to go outside in the dark, that there was something about the moonless night that was eerie and frightening, but that was ridiculous.

"It's so dark. I doubt that I could see anything," was all she could say.

"But you could see the light of the torches if they are coming."

Judith was so worried about Danny that it was impossible to refuse the request, it would have been cruel. But Sharon's heart pounded uncomfortably as she left the room and went towards the back door. In the hall she met Dorothy coming down the stairs.

"I've turned down Judith's bed," she said in a strained voice. "Help me try to persuade her to turn in. She can't do any good just sitting and waiting. She's so tense. It's not good for her . . ."

"I'll be back in a moment. I've promised to look outside and see if I can see any signs of them returning."

She went through the back door into the still, dark garden. Bushes loomed like monsters in the moonless night and the branches of old, thick trees met briefly over her head. She glanced back towards the porch light which she had left on on purpose. The little orange patch was a comforting sight. Her eyes felt heavy from the lack of sleep. That's what's wrong with me, she told herself. I'm jittery from the lack of sleep. Tomorrow she assured herself she would go home with Nick no matter what happened. She would not stay in this place another day no matter how much Brent meant to her. But tomorrow was a long way off—a whole frightening night away.

She made her way across the patio and the lawn towards the back of the house section and there was the garden wall. As she drew near and prepared to stare away into the darkness for sign of the returning men, her heart thumped uncomfortably as a figure moved on the other side. She jammed her fist against her mouth, holding her breath while her eyes tried to get accustomed to the darkness and make out who was on the other side of the wall.

"Who is it?" she whispered, taking a step backwards.

The shadow loomed mightily over her and she laughed aloud with relief. It was a horse. Danny's perhaps. The horse that had wandered home earlier in the evening and had been ignored in the hunt for Danny.

She looked across the paddocks, but there were no lights to be seen. In the dark, eerie night she shivered though the air was warm and turned to go back, glad to be heading for the house and electric lights. She went cold with horror as she bumped into a man standing impassive behind her.

"Oh . . ."

Her head twisted wildly and her body sought an avenue of escape, but the path was narrow and the bushes in the garden on either side would hamper her flight.

"What's the matter?" The voice was quiet, just slightly slurred. It took her a moment to realize that it was Hank, so seldom had she heard him speak.

She controlled her fear determinedly. "What are you doing here, Hank?"

"I've come back for some extra batteries. Two of the torches have given out."

If he touches me I'll scream, she told herself, still trembling.

"And do you expect to find them out here?"

"No. I saw someone in the garden and came down to see if you needed me."

Her heart calmed and stopped thumping. It was ridiculous to be afraid of this quietly-spoken man. After all what was more natural than his excuse for being here? He turned away.

"There's some batteries in the office, Cole said. I'm to get some out of there."

She followed him back towards the

house, becoming calmer as he moved away from her.

"Haven't you found Danny yet?" she asked.

"No."

She waited for him to answer further, but he was a man of few words as well she knew and he said no more.

As though she were afraid to let him out of her sight, she went with him to the office where he found the batteries in just the place Cole had said he would, and saw him leave the house by the back door again.

When he was out of the sight she would have switched off the porch light and gone inside, but, suddenly, it was dark; of its own accord the light flickered out. Blindly, she groped her way inside and the whole house appeared to be in darkness. She felt vulnerable and unprotected in the pitch blackness as though her nameless enemy lurked in the shadows.

"Miss Warden?" she called hesitantly, peering into the dark recesses of the hall.

In front of her the kitchen was suddenly lit with a faint yellow glow and Dorothy appeared in the doorway holding a candlestick in her hand, the flickering light throwing weird shadows over her thin face, mysteriously deepening her haunted eyes.

"What has happened to the lights?" Sharon asked her.

She shrugged in a helpless way and her eyes roved around the hall.

"The plant has broken down or perhaps in their hurry to find Danny the men have forgotten to refuel the tank."

"You have your own power plant?"

"Yes. This happens sometimes."

"What can we do about it?" Sharon did not relish the thought of the dark house with no light other than that afforded by Dorothy's candles.

"We'll just wait. I'm afraid I'm just helpless when it comes to mechanical things. Cole will fix it when he gets back."

"Aunt Dorothy?" It was Judith's voice from the living-room.

"I'm coming my dear."

Sharon followed her. Their shadows were grotesque on the panelled walls. Judith was still in her chair.

"I suppose Cole has forgotten to refuel the tank," she greeted them. "Oh, why don't they come? Surely they've found him by now. Could you see any sign of them coming back?" she asked Sharon who had forgotten about her mission to the back fence in the nervous fear caused by the return of Hank and the failure of the lights.

"No. But Hank came back for some batteries. They haven't found him yet."

Judith twisted her hands in her lap and fell silent. But Dorothy hovered about her. "Please Judith let's go upstairs and try to get some sleep. It's ten o'clock and it sounds as if they'll still be gone for quite a while."

"I can't sleep while Danny is missing."

"Neither can I, but I think you should rest."

"Can you get upstairs without Brent?" Sharon asked in surprise.

"If we help her and she has her sticks," Dorothy answered for Judith.

And as it got later and later and the men did not return they found themselves making that difficult ascent. Sharon was filled with pity that for a moment dispelled the gloom of the night and the sense of foreboding as Judith, painfully heaving herself upwards on her two sticks, supported by Dorothy on one side and Sharon on the other, climbed to the top of the staircase. But even in that clumsy ascent Judith retained a certain grace.

It was after midnight by the time the three women were in their own rooms, intending to sleep if possible until the return of the men.

In her room, Sharon could not go to bed, though she slipped off her frock by the light of a flickering candle and put on a dressing-gown. She thought about Dorothy and Judith and felt sure that they were not sleeping. She could imagine Judith lying awake in her bed, her eyes staring up at the darkened ceiling thinking about Danny. And Dorothy? What was she doing?

For a while Sharon curled up in a bedroom chair fighting an urgent desire for sleep. Despite her anxiety, her head nodded briefly and she dozed for a moment. Then, like an animal sensing danger she convulsed into wakefulness immediately aware of the shadowy room and the silent house.

What am I afraid of? she asked herself.

There's only Judith and Dorothy and me in the house. She had a sudden vision of Hank's dark-clothed figure disappearing into the night. Had he really gone back to the bush or was he lurking outside—or perhaps even inside?

Suddenly the double doors rattled and she sat bolt upright, clutching the arms of the chair. She only relaxed again when she heard the moaning of wind around the house. Then, while she listened, the low growl of a dog. She sat up stiffly. Butch! He was home and Danny must be found.

She moved across and threw open the double doors. She stood on the dark balcony and looked over the railing at the dog on the lawn below, but there was no other sign of life. Gradually she became aware of the other figure that had joined her on the balcony. She turned round slowly. Dorothy was standing a few feet away, her hair whipped away from her face by the brisk wind, her dressing-gown billowing about her legs.

There was that strange, distant expression on her face Sharon knew when she spoke though it was too dark to see it.

"Can you hear it?"

Sharon brushed the question away impatiently. "There's nothing to hear, Miss Warden . . ." But even as she said the words she knew that she was hearing something; from somewhere inside a faint sound.

"What is it?" she asked in a whisper.

"It's a woman crying."

Yes, a woman crying. The unmistakable sound of a woman crying.

"It's Judith," Dorothy said.

"Judith?"

"Yes, she's crying just like she cried that night. She's crying for Brent . . ."

The voice was colourless, monotonous. "You have taken him from her. You are keeping them apart, just as Margaret kept them apart."

She took a step forward and Sharon involuntarily stepped backwards a dreadful, sharp light illuminating her mind. Dorothy advanced towards her slowly and she backed away, frightened by new knowledge and the air of purpose in the woman. She put her hand out behind her feeling for the edge of the balcony and it was cold and smooth beneath her fingers. Dorothy was breathing hard, her face was only a few inches away from Sharon's. Sharon was pressed back against the railing, all her weight was thrown against it. The railing creaked under her weight. There was a loud sound of timber tearing but she did not realize that it had given way until she lost her balance and found she was teetering on the edge of the balcony with nothing between her and the long drop with the hard concrete path at the bottom. A strip of the railing swung out into the night, not quite pulled away from the rest. Her fingers groped out towards Dorothy but she could not get her balance. There was a strangled scream in her throat as she found she was falling, and, even as she fell, she remembered the buzzing and knew what it meant.

With a tremendous effort of will and desire to live and not become a huddled dead or crippled figure on the concrete path, she clutched at the wooden floor of the veranda and, though it seemed her arms must be torn from their sockets, she hung on, digging her slipping fingers in the hard wood. She hung, suspended between two floors, desperately crying to Dorothy for help.

"Please. Please, pull me up. I can't hang on. I can't . . ."

But with dreadful certainty she knew that she could expect no help from Dorothy who had instigated this accident. Oh, Brent, please come back, she cried silently. Beneath her she was aware of the dog growling in his throat as if he, too, could remember another night and was waiting.

Her breath came in hard gasps. "Help me . . ." But she was too weak to cry out loud. Her body dragged on her hands and she could feel her fingers slipping across the wood.

Almost fainting with the pain in her shoulders and shock, she hardly heard Judith's voice.

"Aunt Dorothy, help her. You must. You *must* . . ."

And Dorothy's haunted whisper. "She is going to die like Margaret died. I'm killing her just the way I killed Margaret . . ."

And Judith, almost hysterical. "No, Aunt Dorothy. No! You didn't kill Margaret. Can you hear me? You didn't kill Margaret . . ."

"I didn't?"

"No. Please help her . . ."

Then, miraculously, Dorothy was reaching down, extending arms to draw her up. Sharon mustered all her failing strength. She was aware of distant voices, of footsteps resounding through the house, and she knew that the men had returned. She could faintly discern Judith standing heavily on her sticks just outside her bedroom door as the men poured on to the balcony and more hands reached down to help her. She lay on the floor, panting for breath, nauseated and exhausted while Dorothy leaned over her, solicitous.

18

THEN Brent was helping her to her feet and there were exclamations about the broken balcony rail. She leaned weakly against Brent. But even in her shocked state she looked for Danny and was relieved to see he was there. He looked tired and bedraggled, but he shot past her to Judith, almost colliding with her so that she nearly lost her balance as she leaned heavily on the crutches. Unselfconsciously, she put her arms around him, standing Sharon knew not how, and held the fair head against her.

"Oh, Danny," she murmured through tears. "Where have you been? What happened to you?"

"I got lost in the bush and I couldn't find my way out," he explained.

Over his head her eyes met Brent's. "He's all right, Judith." She smiled weakly at him, ashamed of the tears in her eyes. "You shouldn't be standing up so long," he added, looking at her with that peculiar tenderness he reserved for her alone.

Afterwards Sharon could not remember going downstairs to the living-room but soon they were all there drinking coffee and eating the sandwiches that had been made in preparation for the return of the men. Cole had attended to the lights and Dorothy went to and fro from the kitchen waiting on them all as was her habit, looking strangely composed when one remembered that she had just tried to kill Sharon. Stopping in front of Judith, she asked, "Did you really mean it when you said I didn't kill Margaret?"

The words fell into a sudden pause in the conversation about Danny's disappearance and the accident on the balcony. There was a self-conscious silence as though each one knew that this must be the showdown.

Judith looked about the room as if she wanted to be sure that everyone was present and would hear what she had to say. "Yes, I did mean it, Aunt Dorothy. You didn't kill Margaret. Have you really thought that you did?"

Dorothy nodded dumbly, her expression confused.

"I should have told the truth at the beginning," Judith went on, "and then perhaps none of this would have happened. But I thought I was doing the right thing at the time." She stared at Brent as if the words were for his ears alone.

He went and sat down beside her, suddenly taking one of her hands in his. "Who did kill Margaret?" he asked her quietly.

Her eyes turned to hold his again. "She killed herself, Brent. She tried to push me off the balcony. I . . . I hung on to her to save myself when I found I was falling and . . . we both fell." She waited for him to speak but he said nothing. "Oh, Brent, don't you see. I couldn't tell everyone what really happened that night. You would have hated it, the awful publicity, everybody knowing. It would have been in the papers. It was so ugly. She tried to kill me because I had taken her husband . . ." She turned violently away and covered her eyes with her hands. "You were too proud to have your name bandied around in a scandal of that kind. I thought it best to say that she had apparently had one of her turns and fallen against the rotted railing and that when I tried to prevent her falling she pulled me with her. I know now I should have told the truth then."

There was a stranger expression in Brent's eyes as though some great truth had been revealed to him. Judith went on, "You do believe me, Brent? I know I've lied, but this is the truth. You do believe me, don't you?"

He nodded slowly. "Yes, I believe you." And Sharon also believed her and was convinced that this was the truth about Margaret's death. But why had Dorothy attempted to kill her and who had written the notes? There were so many questions.

Dorothy her eyes bright, her hair awry, patted Sharon on the hand. "You must forgive me, my dear. I might have killed you."

"Why did you do it, Miss Warden?" Sharon asked her intensely.

She shrugged, and looked about the room. Everyone was present except Danny who had been bundled off to bed. But, as though this were the time for truth and it must all be understood now, she said, "For Judith. To stop you marrying Brent. At first I just tried to frighten you away with a note, but then you and Brent planned to marry and I thought I would have to kill you . . ."

"You mean you wrote me the note, and the ones to Margaret?"

"Yes. And when Margaret ignored them I thought I would have to kill her." For a moment, she held her hand against her eyes and reeled back on her heels. Sharon put out a hand to steady her. "I . . . I thought I had killed her," she whispered. "That's what I couldn't remember. That I had killed her. I remember now. I didn't know that I wrote the notes until just now." She stared at Sharon. "Isn't that strange? I didn't know I wrote the notes. I'm all mixed up. There were the two days you see. The day that Margaret died and today." Her eyes widened as if she looked at something in the past that no one else could see. "The day that Margaret died she quarrelled with Judith. Oh, they thought they were alone, but I was listening. She called Judith a . . . a . . . slut. Can you imagine? Judith." Out of the corner of her eyes Sharon saw Brent's grip on Judith's hand tighten. "She said she would never give Brent up, never. And that night I heard Judith crying. She was crying just like tonight. I . . . I couldn't bear it . . ."

Brent stared down at Judith's bent head. She kept her gaze averted.

"What happened then?" Sharon prompted.

"The dog barked. Yes, that's right, the dog barked. I went out on to the balcony to shush him. Judith and Margaret went out too. They were standing by the rail, leaning over the rail . . ."

"Yes?"

"I didn't see just what happened. I was standing there thinking to myself how easy it would be to push Margaret. I knew the boards were rotten. I had noticed the day before that they were eaten away and I was going to tell Brent about it. I had an irresistible urge to push Margaret, and, then, all I remember is that she was falling and screaming . . . And Judith. I . . . I thought I had pushed her. I thought I had killed her and crippled Judith . . ."

Then, as if she could remain coherent

no longer, she burst into violent weeping. Sharon led her to a chair. She patted her on the shoulder. "Don't cry, Miss Warden. Please, don't cry . . ."

But Dorothy sat bolt upright. "No, I must tell you all of it," she went on. "Today I heard Judith beg you to give Brent up . . ."

Sharon coloured violently but Judith sat absolutely still, looking down at Brent's hand clasping her own.

"And tonight I could hear her crying in her room. And the dog was growling and you were on the balcony. It was almost as if you were Margaret come back . . ." She looked around the room with wide eyes. "But just in time Judith came and told me I hadn't killed Margaret, and I didn't want to kill anyone . . . I was free . . ."

Her voice trailed off as if she were talking only to herself.

"But someone tried to shoot me this morning," Sharon murmured, bewildered. "It couldn't have been you Miss Warden. And did you come into my room when I was sleeping . . . ?"

She broke off in confusion, looking helplessly round at the group.

Cole was leaning against the wall, listening to it all, his eyes half-closed. Now, he stood up straight and moved into the centre of the room.

"Okay, okay," he said. "I'll come clean too. I cannot tell a lie, I did it with my little hatchet," he mocked.

Brent stood up. "What are you talking about, Cole?"

"Just like I said. I fired a shot this morning in the direction of the lady."

"You mean you tried to kill me?" Sharon gasped.

He bowed in her direction. "If I had tried to kill you you would be dead," he said. "I never miss the target. I was aimin' at the tree and that's what I hit."

"But what for?"

"To give that skunk George Paxton a fright that's why. And that's why I was in your room. I wanted to look through Margaret's letters, but I knew Brent wouldn't let me. You were sleeping in Margaret's room and her letters were in the desk in there. I climbed up over the balcony and helped myself to some of them. I just wanted something to pin on

296

that critter." His lip curled. "And I found it."

Brent moved across to him, his face blazing with anger and for a moment Sharon thought he was going to hit Cole. How little I know him, she thought afterwards. He would never resort to violence. And I even thought he was capable of murder.

"You're a damn fool, Cole," Brent said evenly. "I should turn you over to the police and see if they can knock some sense into you."

Cole swayed on his feet, his thumbs hooked in his belt. "Brent Warden, the big shot. Brent Warden, the big landowner."

"That's always annoyed you, hasn't it, Cole? That I own Warden's Cove? You've hated me for that. Well, there's something you should know. Just before Dad died he told me the terms of the will. I was to get Warden's Cove, but, if you ever showed any signs of maturity and I thought you were worthy of the place, he wanted me to share it with you. But the onus was on me. The choice was to be mine. All right, you and Hank do the hard work around the place as you're so fond of telling me, and it seemed to me only just that you should have some reward. How old are you? You'll be twenty-five in May I believe. The lawyers are drawing up the papers now to give you part of the property on your twenty-fifth birthday. But, God knows, I feel I'm making a mistake. You'll never grow up. You certainly don't show any signs of maturity."

Watching Cole, Sharon saw a remarkable change come over his features as he listened. The hard veneer seemed to melt a little, he looked more natural than he ever had. There was something in his face that reminded her of a child at Christmas.

Brent's voice rose. "You've got to May to prove that I'm not making a mistake, Cole. One damned fool action out of you between now and then and I'll cancel the transfer."

But Sharon did not think that Brent would have any more trouble with Cole.

They were interrupted by the diversion of Dorothy falling asleep in the chair, exhausted. There was a murmur of voices saying that she must go to bed.

"She must be very very tired," Brent

said, quietly. "She really hasn't slept very well for a year. I'll phone Alan Matthews and ask him to come out as soon as possible in case she needs medical attention of any kind."

They were all tired and the gathering began to break up as they drifted off to bed for what was left of the night. But Sharon still seethed with unanswered questions and half-formulated answers and she could not wait until the morning to settle her doubts. And so she waited for an opportunity to catch Brent alone when the others had all retired to their beds. He was downstairs putting out the lights when she accosted him.

"You haven't turned in," he greeted her in some surprise, but she knew straight away that he was wary of her. But why? There's no reason now, Brent, to be aloof with me, she thought. There's nothing to hide, nothing to be afraid of.

"I want to talk to you."

"You're a terror for wanting to talk," he said, suddenly smiling slightly and her spirits rose. She smiled back.

"I've still got lots of questions to ask," she rejoined, in the same light mood.

His smile faded. "What is it you want to know now?"

"Brent why did you try to hide the circumstances of Margaret's death from me when you didn't know who did it?" He did not reply and she gritted her teeth and went on, "You thought that Judith had pushed Margaret off the balcony, didn't you? You thought that Judith had murdered your wife." Still, he was silent and she knew she was right. "Oh, it explains so much. It explains why you wanted me to go home, why you said it would be dangerous for me to stay. You thought Judith might attempt to murder me. And it explains why you weren't a bit concerned when Cole shot at me. You knew Judith couldn't fire a gun. You really believed that Cole or Hank was trying to shoot a rabbit. And it explains why you've treated Judith so coldly. You felt guilty. And why you didn't marry her when you were both free. You couldn't bring yourself to marry a murderess. She really went down in your estimation. But, why, why did you propose to me?"

She thought he was not going to answer her again, but, after a long pause, weighing his words, carefully, he said, "The whole affair was so vile. Such violence was repulsive to me. I went away to be rid of the guilt and disgust and I met you. You are good through and through, and clean. There was something about you that reminded me of being in the open air. If I could be with you for the rest of my life I thought I would be cleansed, I could forget the whole horrible business. But the night that I was supposed to meet your parents, I couldn't do it because, though one half of me wanted you, sweet and uncomplicated, the other kept nagging at me, telling me that I really loved Judith; that despite what she had done, I still loved her."

"Oh, Brent . . ." How astute Cole had been. How strange that he should have seen so clearly Brent's motives.

"I'm sorry, Sharon. I can't help it. I still love her now. I can't forgive myself for what I've done to you. When you appeared here and I was back in the atmosphere of Warden's Cove, I was carried away again by my guilt and your goodness. I asked you to marry me, but it's no good, Sharon.

I can't marry anyone but Judith. I must ask you to release me . . ."

Shocked almost out of control, she interrupted him. "Oh, Brent, please don't talk about it now. Wait until the morning."

She turned blindly away towards the stairs.

"Sharon . . ."

She turned back, hope rising, her face alight.

"I'm sorry . . ."

Feeling as though her whole body ached with unshed tears she fled from him up the stairs to her room. Without knowing what she did she prepared for bed and, when she lay between the sheets, could not even appreciate that, for what was left of this night, she could relax and sleep unafraid. She did not even need to jam the chair beneath the door handle. The success of her efforts to unravel the mystery of Margaret's death left a bitter taste in her mouth. For with success she had lost what she wanted most. For she knew that in the morning she would have to control herself and make a graceful exit from Warden's Cove and from Brent's life.

19

IT was a lovely summer day with just a hint of autumn in the clear air. At about nine-thirty she was on the wharf waiting for Nick's boat to appear around the headland. One by one the family had tried to persuade her to wait until he reappeared in the evening, but, now, she was impatient to be gone. It seemed to her that Brent's attempt to delay her was half-hearted and she felt she could not be free of Warden's Cove soon enough. And it was humiliating to be there now that they all knew there was to be no marriage. She had saved her pride, she hoped, by announcing in a casual manner that she would not be coming back, that she felt she had made a mistake and the marraige was off. Nobody seemed particularly surprised though Judith's eyes seemed to glow, a radiance tinged with sympathy, and Sharon decided that Brent had already made a confession to her. But, being a gentleman, she told herself, ironically, he will wait a while until he tells everyone else that he is in love with her.

Brent and Danny had come down to the jetty to see her off and she was glad to see Nick's boat appear right on time. Though it would take him a while to anchor at the jetty she collected up her suitcase and clutched it, moving to where she knew the boat would dock.

"Let me take that," Brent said, taking it from her.

She waited awkwardly, anxious to get the good-byes said.

"Good-bye, Brent. I hope you and Judith will be very happy."

"That's very generous of you."

She could see he was really feeling contrite. She forced a smile. "Don't worry about me. Now, don't start getting a guilt complex about *me*."

"I feel very badly about it."

"I'll be all right. I'm used to it," she added, with pathetic irony. "I told you about my sister, didn't I?" She was talking too brightly, saying things she had no intention of saying. She changed the subject abruptly. "I hope Miss Warden will be all right."

"She will now, I think. Alan Matthews will be out to see her today." He shook his head thinking about Aunt Dorothy, glad to be on safer conversational ground. "Such a strange story. I had a look at the balcony this morning. Do you know she had actually sawn through the railing so that you would lean on it and fall."

"Yes, I know. I heard her early last night. And when I fell the noise came back to me. But it was all so clumsy. How could she think she would get away with a murder like that?"

"She didn't think in terms of getting away with it. Her other self did it. It was a sort of compulsion to get for Judith what she wanted. Poor Aunt Dorothy. She's been living under a dreadful strain. Though she was like two people and her normal self didn't know what the other self was doing, her subconscious mind believed her to be a murderess. She wanted so much to forget what she thought she had done, that she just couldn't remember it. This morning she knows nothing about the sawn balcony rail. I'll get Cole to repair it and nothing need be said about it."

Yes, she thought, Cole will repair it.

Brent would be incapable of it. He's really rather helpless. But he'll make Judith happy. He's the man she needs.

Her irrepressible curiosity began to assert itself as the *Louise* neared the jetty and she knew that soon, now, she would not be able to ask any more more questions of him.

"Brent," she began, "why did you tell Danny not to tell the police about the third person on the balcony? There was another person . . ."

"It was Aunt Dorothy I suppose," he agreed. "She witnessed the whole thing. Did I tell him not to mention it?"

"Danny thinks you did."

"Perhaps I did. I wanted to keep the whole thing as simple as possible not to raise the police's suspicions. If he'd come out with a thing like that it might have opened up whole avenues of thought. And no one admitted to being on the balcony. I didn't want to give the police any reasons for carrying their investigations further. It might have led to Judith . . ." He looked at her intently. "You must forgive Aunt Dorothy. What she did she did because she loves Judith more than herself. Her only crime is that she loves Judith too much."

"Can it ever be a crime to love anyone too much?"

Then the *Louise* had docked and there was a confusion of helloes and good-byes and, almost before she knew it, she was standing in the cockpit and Nick was at the wheel and the *Louise* was heading again for the open sea. Brent and Danny stood on the jetty and watched it leave, Dorothy appeared briefly at the gate of the homestead, waving a frantic good-bye and, just before they rounded the next bend and the cove could not be seen, two horsemen, Cole and Hank, appeared on the horizon. They saluted casually.

She stood for a long time looking over the water and was unaware of the scrutiny she had from Nick. Then she turned back into the cockpit and sat down, adjusting her wide-brimmed hat.

"You look rather shaken," he said at last. "Are you all right?"

"Yes."

He wants an explanation, of course, she thought. I've told him so much and now he wants to know how it all turned out.

But she was reluctant to talk about it and was silent for a long time. But he was a patient man who minded his own business and so he worked on his boat and said nothing more, giving her time to compose herself.

And so they did not talk about Warden's Cove until that afternoon when they were on the return run and the *Louise* passed by the farm again.

"That's the last time I'll see Warden's Cove," she said, and did not notice the flare of interest in his expression.

"You're not going back?" he asked with careful nonchalance.

"No."

"Do you want to tell me why?"

"Because I am not going to marry Brent," she said with forced brightness.

"You turned him down?"

She would have liked to leave it at that, but she could not lie, specially to him.

"No, he turned me down. He wants to marry Judith. Everyone was right you see. He was in love with her all the time."

He looked at her searchingly and saw the proud lift of her head and the heartache underneath. "I'm sorry."

"I'm used to it," she said flippantly. "I have a very beautiful sister. Have I told you about my sister? She has often taken my boy-friends. I seem to make a habit of losing out to more beautiful women. Kerry is really something. You'd go for her."

"Would I?" He was not flippant; he was very serious.

She looked away. "But I ruined my own romance this time. I killed it with my stupid curiosity. If I'd just let matters be, Brent would have married me. He thought Judith had killed Margaret, and I was just an outlet apparently, a sort of comforting salve for his conscience." Rather hesitantly she told him about the night before and it was typical of him that he did not interrupt but heard her out.

"It seems," she explained, "that Miss Warden intended to frighten Margaret into giving Brent a divorce with some threatening notes she kept writing, but, when Margaret took no notice of them, she made up her mind to kill her. She loves Judith so much that she was just determined that Judith should have what she wanted: Brent. On the day that Margaret died, she heard Margaret and Judith quarrelling and

Judith begging her to set Brent free. Margaret apparently called Judith some pretty awful names and that night Dorothy who slept next door to Judith heard Judith crying. Then the dog barked and Dorothy went out on to the balcony. She knew the wood had rotted and there was Margaret leaning over the rail calling out to Butch to be quiet. Dorothy knew that was her opportunity but as she still stood in the doorway, Judith also came out on to the balcony and another argument developed. It seems that Margaret tried to push Judith off and Judith clung to her and fell too. Poor Dorothy in a state of almost unbearable tension, all geared to kill Margaret, thought she had pushed Margaret off and maimed Judith. She was so horrified at what she thought she had done to Judith particularly that something clicked in her head and she just couldn't remember any of it. But every time the dog howled at night she was on the verge of remembering. And she would go out on to the balcony almost in a trance, listening for Judith crying. And when she saw Brent about to marry me and the situation repeating itself, she started all over again, writing the notes, subconsciously planning to murder me. And she nearly did. She would have done it if Judith hadn't told her that she didn't kill Margaret. That was such a relief to her that she lost all interest in killing me . . ."

She told him all she knew trying to explain the people at Warden's Cove and their part in the terrifying few days through which she had lived.

"Some of the time I was inventing trouble," she told him. "I was seeing shadows that I thought were a person watching, following me. That night I came down to the *Louise* I felt sure someone watched me from a window. And I read such significance into small things; the way Judith was so worried about what George knew. It was natural for her to be worried. She knew what he was like. She is fond of the family and she wouldn't want them hurt . . ."

Te Kiri Bay came into sight. What a long time it seemed since she had seen it last. There was the jetty jutting out into the sea, the small sea-craft, the sandy beach, the toi tois. And winding up from the beach was the road into Te Kiri, the few shops, the hotel, the scattered houses. From here only a few days earlier she had left full of determination and hope. But now she felt dead, emotionless. Brent was gone and there was nothing left. To-morrow she would leave for home and life would be as it had been before she had met him.

20

IT was a night like that other mellow summer night. Sharon was weeding the flower-beds along the front of the house. She sat back on her heels and glanced, for a moment, at the family taking the cooler air on the porch. It was just as it had been that other night and, briefly, her senses reeled. A whole year had gone by and everything, on the surface, was just the same. But she would never be the same again.

A long, hard year had passed. A year of pretending; putting on a face for the rest of the family; a year of trying to forget. A year of desperate, unsatisfied need.

She stood up and brushed the dirt from her hands and looked with approval at the neat, weed-free garden. Gardening was so rewarding. The garden reminded her of Dorothy and she sighed audibly thinking of the family at Warden's Cove, wondering about them. There was a thoughtful, distant expression in her eyes though she was unaware of it.

She went inside to wash her hands and clean up a little, and was at the wash-basin in the bathroom when her mother came quietly in behind her. Their eyes met in the mirror over the basin. Sharon knew instinctively that she was in for a period of questioning and she mentally prepared herself for it.

"Sharon, why won't you tell me what's the matter?"

"The matter?"

"Yes. You're not happy. I can tell. I'm your mother."

"I'm all right."

"No, you're not. Something has been very wrong since . . . since that last holiday . . . When you went away just after . . . what was his name? . . . Brent Warden didn't turn up that night."

Sharon dried her hands with careful attention to detail, playing for time but aware that she would have to make some sort of confession to her mother. She owed her that much.

"Don't worry about me," she said at last.

"I can't help worrying about you."

"All right. The truth is that I loved him and, when I went away that time, I visited him at his home and found out that he didn't love me. There was another girl and he had just been having a holiday-flirtation. Does that answer your questions?"

"I suppose so. But what about you?"

"I've got over it now."

"Are you sure?"

She thought about it. Was she sure? It was a certain fact that time gradually healed. One couldn't go on forever loving a person who loved someone else. Brent had shattered her self respect and that was enough to weaken her love.

"Shall we go back on the porch in the fresh air? It's so hot in here," she suggested to change the subject.

As they arrived on the porch, she was surprised to see a long, blue car pull up at the kerb. They looked at one another wondering who it could be. A man climbed out of the driver's seat and stood on the side of the road, slamming shut the door. It did not immediately register who

315

he was, and when it did she could not believe her own eyes.

"Nick!" she said.

The family were all looking at her and she found the colour rising in her face. She stared at him. He was unfamiliar in a correct suit. Over the top of the car he grinned and saluted her with his free hand.

For the first time in a year, she felt alive, interested, even excited.

"Nick!" she said again and flew down the steps to meet him. They met on the kerb, and suddenly, she was just a little shy. She put both her hands behind her like a child. "You're all dressed up," she said in confusion.

"I do sometimes."

"What?"

"Dress up."

"Oh . . ." She led him up the steps towards the waiting group on the porch.

"This is my mother." He shook hands. "And my father. This is Nick Kane. And this is my sister, Kerry . . ." There was an interested gleam in Kerry's eye as Sharon looked at her, but it did not worry her this time. She looked at Nick and she was not afraid that Kerry would attract his

316

interest. She had never mentioned him to the family and now she found it difficult to explain him.

"Why don't you go inside and change, dear?" her mother suggested and she looked down at her denim jeans and brief blouse. But, again, she was not worried that Nick had found her untidy. She pushed her unruly hair back off her face.

"I'm all right," she said.

The daylight was fading and they moved into the house. He was completely relaxed, apparently at home, sitting in a lounge chair in the living-room. He talked easily with her father, and was deferential to her mother. He did not seem to notice Kerry's cool appraisal and paid her only the attention that good manners demanded. Ironically Sharon thought of a year ago and how this was what she had expected of Brent.

About ten o'clock Mrs. Denholm announced that she would make a cup of coffee.

"I'll make it," Sharon offered and retired to the kitchen where each member of the family found an excuse to be in the next few minutes.

"Sharon, where did you dig him up?

He's neat," Kerry sighed in unfeigned admiration.

It was quite a usual attitude of Kerry's but this time it amused Sharon. She was surprised to find herself laughing lightly and realized, with a jolt, that she felt vaguely happy for the first time in a year.

"I met him when I was away last year."

"You mean you've had him hidden all this time and you didn't tell us. Is he the one who was supposed to come here to meet us that night?"

"Of course not. If Nick had said he would come, he would have come. That's what he's like."

"He's gone on you. Are you going to get married?"

Sharon did not answer immediately. Obviously Nick had come for a purpose and she was going to have to face the issue. She found herself thinking about marriage to Nick and the idea was not unattractive.

"Are you?" Kerry asked again. "He'd make a terrific husband."

"How do you know? You've only just met him."

"I can tell. Gee, I wish he'd come to see *me*."

Kerry's enthusiasm did a lot to lift the bitterness Sharon had often felt towards her in the past. The times I lost out to Kerry in the past were probably my own fault in a way, she told herself. I expected to lose out.

After Kerry came her mother.

"My dear, you didn't tell us about him. Not a word have you said . . ."

"There was nothing to tell . . ."

"Oh, but I can see there is. He has a certain look about him . . ."

"Would you like to carry the sandwiches in for me?" Sharon interrupted and hustled her out.

Even Bob Denholm could not resist wandering into the kitchen.

"Now, this young man, Sharon . . ."

"Yes, Dad?"

"There's a bit of Maori there, I'd say."

"Yes, there is."

She waited for what he would say next, surprised to find that her heart was racing with anxiety for Nick. She felt fiercely protective. If there were any criticism of Nick at all she would lose her temper, she knew it. And it rather shocked her. How strange. It had always been there; a possessive emotion about him; as though he were hers and she would see no fault in him.

"You'll just have to be very sure before you get to marrying him," was all her father said.

"It doesn't make any difference."

"I know. I know. Absolute equality and all that. But there are people who let it make a difference. You've got to think of the children."

"I'll teach them to be proud of it; that they're superior because of it. Children always believe the things their parents tell them." She smiled lightly and kissed him on the forehead. "The colour bar in reverse. Then no matter how the world treats them they'll always believe that other people are secretly jealous!"

She stopped, aware, for the first time, that she was talking as if marriage to Nick was an accepted fact, and her face was thoughtful.

Immediately after supper the family drifted off to bed and she was left alone with Nick. She sat on the couch opposite him, her eyes dancing.

"We are being left alone," she said.

"That's very kind of them." He studied her for a moment. "I suppose you want to know all about the Wardens."

She knew he meant Brent and she wanted to protest that she was not interested, but she could not. She *did* want to know.

"Have you seen them much?"

"Usually every two or three days. Brent and Judith are married," he added, abruptly.

Her gaze did not falter. "I presumed they would be. And did it cause any talk?"

"A bit. Not enough to cause any more speculation about Margaret's death."

"So for Judith it ended happy ever after. Even being crippled won't spoil it for her. She doesn't need to walk. She's got Brent and Dorothy."

"Dorothy went away for a spell. A rest home."

"Poor Aunt Dorothy. Did it all come out?"

"No. The Wardens are very close. They kept the whole thing to themselves. Doctor Matthews and I are the only other people who know anything about it. Dorothy is home again. Just a bit too bright but nothing very much. I notice the Te Kiri folk are talking a lot less about the Wardens than they did. The whole business is just dying a natural death. Even Cole is behaving himself."

Yes, she thought, they needn't worry about Cole any more. He would be good now that he had got what he had really wanted all the time; a part of Warden's Cove. And she was glad of that because it meant that she did not have to worry about his antagonism towards Nick.

The conversation was running out and she held her breath. He moved across to the couch and sat down beside her and she was terribly conscious of him.

"Why have you come, Nick?" she asked at last.

"You know why, Sharon. To ask you to marry me, what else?"

She turned to face him.

"But Nick, why now? I mean . . . you haven't seen me for a year . . ."

"I waited to give you time to get over Brent."

She thought of earlier in the evening when she had told herself that one just couldn't go on loving a person who loved someone else. Perhaps there were, after all, some people who were capable of persistent, unrewarded devotion.

"Have you got over him?"

She tried hard to be honest, to assess exactly how she felt about Brent.

"I don't think I'll ever really get over him," she said. "I've been so horribly hurt. But I don't think I . . . have any love left for him either . . . I just don't know, Nick. I just don't know . . ."

"Let's get married anyway . . ."

"You mean you still want me under those circumstances . . . ?"

"Under any circumstances. Say yes and we'll take the *Louise* to Australia for our honeymoon. You're the only girl I've ever met that could compete with the *Louise* for my affections . . ." He smiled to make her respond.

She thought about the *Louise* and saw it clearly against a backdrop of sea and sky. The life he led seemed very appealing; different and carefree and she liked to think of herself as part of it. She wondered if she could trust this strange, unfamiliar happiness.

Her smile flashed briefly. She put both

323

arms loosely around his neck and kissed him experimentally.

"Nick, I like to think of being married to you. It would be fun. And I've been so proud of you tonight, showing you off to my family. And they like you. I can tell. And always, even when I was so much in love with Brent, I felt as if you and I belonged together. I'd like to have your children, Nick. A dark little boy who looks like his father and a little girl with big brown eyes . . ." She kissed him again. "That's all I can say for sure now. Is that enough to start on?"

"That's pretty good for a start," he said.

THE END

GUIDE
TO THE COLOUR CODING
OF
ULVERSCROFT BOOKS

Many of our readers have written to us expressing their appreciation for the way in which our colour coding has assisted them in selecting the Ulverscroft books of their choice.

To remind everyone of our colour coding— this is as follows:

BLACK COVERS
Mysteries

★

BLUE COVERS
Romances

★

RED COVERS
Adventure Suspense and General Fiction

★

ORANGE COVERS
Westerns

★

GREEN COVERS
Non-Fiction